Val's Prayer

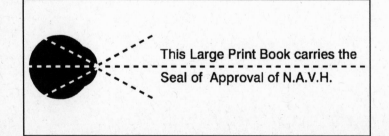

This Large Print Book carries the
Seal of Approval of N.A.V.H.

VAL'S PRAYER

TERRY FOWLER

THORNDIKE PRESS
A part of Gale, Cengage Learning

GALE
CENGAGE Learning®

Detroit • New York • San Francisco • New Haven, Conn • Waterville, Maine • London

GALE
CENGAGE Learning®

LIBRARY OF CONGRESS CATALOGING-IN-PUBLICATION DATA

Fowler, Terry.
  Val's prayer / by Terry Fowler. — Large print ed.
    p. cm. — (Thorndike Press large print Christian fiction)
  "Kentucky Weddings Series; #1.
    ISBN 978-1-4104-4483-7 (hardcover) — ISBN 1-4104-4483-X (hardcover)
  1. Businesswomen—Fiction. 2. Architects—Fiction. 3. Horse farms—Fiction. 4. Kentucky—Fiction. 5. Large type books. I. Title.
PS3556.O86V35 2012
813'.54—dc23   2011047815

Published in 2012 by arrangement with Barbour Publishing, Inc.

Printed in Mexico
1 2 3 4 5 6 7 16 15 14 13 12

To My Savior — who makes
all things possible.
To my friends Mary and Steve —
thanks for introducing me
to your Kentucky.
To my family — I love you all.

ONE

"Why are you doing this?"

Val Truelove studied the man with interest. When she had spoken with Randall King of Prestige Designs earlier in the week, he'd said they would be in contact; and then yesterday Russell Hunter had called to schedule the appointment. His eagerness to work together seemed to have taken a three-sixty turn today.

For some reason known only to him, Russell Hunter had become annoyed when she outlined the job. Val considered that strange since she'd given him the same information she'd given his employer. Surely Mr. King had told him what she planned.

Handsome, confident, and well dressed, with the most piercing blue eyes and somber expression — Val wondered if he ever smiled. He looked to be around her age but acted much older. Struggling to maintain her cool even though her defense mechanism had kicked in, Val asked, "Do you always question your client's reason for a project?"

"Yours is an unusual request."

Val didn't doubt that for a moment. "The structure is part of the business I plan to run here at Sheridan Farm."

"What business?" he demanded. "This is a Kentucky horse farm. Will's Shadow put this place on the map."

He hadn't told Val anything she didn't already know. In fact, her father, Jacob Truelove, had played a major role in the breeding and training of that very same horse.

"Will's Shadow has moved on to greener pastures, and I have other plans for part of the acreage. I'm opening Your Wedding Place."

"Your Wedding Place?" he repeated. "You mean like those wedding chapels in Vegas?"

"No. Nothing like that." Placing her hands on the desk, Val pushed herself to her feet. "This isn't going to work. I don't need an architect who acts more like a prosecuting attorney."

Russ stood and straightened his suit coat. "I have a right to care about changes that affect our community. My family owns

Hunter Farm."

"And yet you diversified." At his puzzled expression she said, "You chose architecture."

"My brother inherited the farm."

"And that makes you angry about my project?"

"You'd be upset if your birthright had been stolen."

She shrugged, wondering how he connected the two. "Things come and go. I consider my good name, morals, and values to be the only worthwhile birthright I have."

He grimaced and exclaimed, "Never mind. It's not something I care to discuss. We were talking about what you're doing to this community."

"I'm paying the previous owner a considerable sum that gives me the right to do whatever I want. And there aren't any provisos that I have to seek anyone's permission to do so."

"I think the zoning board might have something to say about that."

Had he just threatened her? His negative reaction stirred Val's underlying concern about her plans. Was she doing the right thing? Yes. He was wrong, she told herself. Your Wedding Place would be a success. Paris was just minutes outside Lexington.

Brides would come from all over once they heard about the perfect venue for their weddings.

"There's a lot less farmland and more than one shopping center or housing development on what used to be Kentucky horse farms," Val told him. "And from what I can see, people aren't avoiding the shopping or living accommodations because you don't like change."

"I wouldn't expect you to understand. You have no idea what it's like to live on a horse farm."

Wrong again, Val thought. She had grown up right here at Sheridan Farm in the house provided for the general manager's family. When the elder Mr. Sheridan passed away and left the property to his son, they had run the farm with the absentee owner rarely stopping by to check on his inheritance.

Her respect for the farm had grown over the years, and even though she'd spent the past seven years working as an assistant to a wedding planner in Lexington, Val fully understood what it meant to her family.

She also believed God had provided her this opportunity. In the course of her work she had spent hours searching for wedding venues and believed a business offering multiple location choices would be a profit maker. But the expense involved made the project an impossible dream — until now. "Sheridan Farm is big enough to support more than one business."

"It's a horse farm."

"You obviously don't share my vision, so let's just call it quits before one of us says something we'll regret."

Russ drew a deep breath. His boss had warned him about antagonizing the clients. Randall King had been very clear about the outcome last week when Russ had nearly lost a very solvent account in practically the same manner. He would learn to keep his opinions to himself or be without a job. Yet he'd just managed to irritate another potential client.

Val Truelove had a smile on her face and a welcome in her voice when she had invited him into William Sheridan's office. Now she was seconds from throwing him out. The idea of begging her forgiveness galled Russ, but he couldn't afford to lose his time investment in Prestige Designs. He was too close to completing his internship. His plan to have his own business by thirty had already been delayed when he'd wasted those years after his parents' death.

"I'm sorry, Ms. Truelove." What kind of

name was that anyway? "You're right. Life moves on whether we want it to or not. Tell me more about this structure you want to build."

Russ Hunter had learned a few things about women in his twenty-seven years and was not above flirting to get his way. He flashed a smile he hoped would make a two-hundred-watt bulb look dim. "Please give me another chance. And call me Russ."

Small and petite, she'd seemed lost behind the massive desk. Her long brown hair hung straight, golden highlights gleaming in the sunlight that streamed through the bank of windows directly behind her. She'd obviously made some effort with her appearance though the jeans and long-sleeved black top looked worn and definitely off the rack. Her features were just irregular enough to keep her from stunning beauty, but still Russ found her to be an arresting woman.

"Val," she said before sitting down. "All I want is to see the work underway. I don't care who creates the plans, but I do find it difficult to believe you can accomplish this when you obviously have problems with my converting Kentucky countryside for my schemes."

He had insulted her. "I'm one of the best architects around," Russ declared proudly.

"It just happens that I have a mouth big enough to hold the hooves of more than one thoroughbred. Not to mention I'm too opinionated for my own good. I've created a number of designs for Prestige Designs. I'd be happy to provide you with my portfolio."

"That's not necessary. I don't doubt your qualifications. And if you can agree to keep an open mind I'm willing to try to make this work."

Russ nodded. "I'd like an opportunity to prove I'm capable of giving you what you want."

She eyed him for a moment longer before she said, "Okay. Here's what I have in mind."

He listened as she outlined the structure that would be used for outdoor receptions during the spring and summer months. Russ could tell she'd given the matter a great deal of thought.

"I don't know if the technical description would be colonnade or pavilion. It would be ideal if we could find a way to enclose it for fall and winter, but I suspect we'll need yet another building at a later date."

"Just how big are you planning to make this structure?" Russ asked, imagining something that put a football stadium to shame.

Val turned to reach for a stack of papers on the credenza. "I'd like to have room for three hundred people. The project goes far beyond this construction. What I need from you is a long-range plan I can continue to develop as Your Wedding Place grows. Along with the twenty-five acres, I've included the house and gardens in this project."

"For parties?" he repeated, disbelief trickling back into his tone.

She shrugged. "I suppose we might host the occasional social event. But first and foremost, Your Wedding Place will become the premier location where every bride can hold the wedding of her dreams."

She pulled a piece of foamboard onto the desktop. Shielding her plans from view, Val said, "Before I share these, you must agree to keep my ideas confidential."

"Yes," he said with a nod. "Prestige Designs guarantees complete confidentiality of all their work."

The plans she showed him, while the work of an amateur, demonstrated great promise. She'd cleverly laid out her ideas. Phase one involved the possible conversion of the main house to a bed-and-breakfast with plans to improve the existing gardens to use as individual venues. He counted four areas — English, Japanese, formal, and the informal front garden.

Her board indicated the construction of this structure as part of the second phase, but apparently she'd moved it up in priority. She had plans for more gardens, structures, even an inn, restaurant, and bakery. Russ found it mind-boggling to say the least.

"What are these?" he asked, indicating what appeared to be roadways throughout the projects.

"Carriage trails. See, Mr. Hunter . . . uh, Russ . . . I don't intend to forget the horses."

"You're going to use the finest horseflesh in the world to pull carriages?" As soon as the words slipped out, Russ winced. It would take a miracle for him to keep this client and his job.

"Don't be silly."

Russ knew the value of a good horse. Why was it silly to assume she planned to use animals that had been born and bred with the intent of making them Triple Crown winners?

"Even I know you don't use a racehorse to pull a carriage. My father will find the animals. I'm building trails, not racetracks."

"And you have the finances to make all this happen?"

"You're doing it again," she pointed out.

"I'm sorry," Russ said, indicating the board he held. "These are the plans of a major development company. I'm curious as to how it's possible one person could afford such a project."

"Let's just say my ship came in," she said with a tiny smile.

Certainly no dinghy, Russ thought. "So where do we start?"

"At the beginning," Val answered easily. "As I said, I want plans I can develop long term. We'll start small, four venues. This is the first structure I want completed. I need a place for receptions."

"Can I take this with me?" Russ asked.

Val shook her head. "That's my project board. I have a list, though, outlining what I want from you."

"Perfect. I'll take it back to the office and get back to you within the week."

"The sooner this structure is completed and earning a profit, the sooner I can move forward with my next project."

He accepted the folder she handed him. "I understand. It's been a pleasure meeting you, Ms. Truelove . . . Val."

"I doubt it's been the highlight of your day," she told him. "But if you're willing to design a project worthy of your portfolio,

I'm sure we'll find the arrangement mutually beneficial."

Russ removed a business card from his briefcase and placed it in the center of the desk. "I accept your challenge and look forward to proving myself."

"Would you like to see the site I have in mind?"

After they completed a brief tour, Russ said he would be in touch. Outside the house, he started his car and gunned the engine, tires spinning in the marl as he drove toward the main highway. Life wasn't fair. How could she afford this?

Val Truelove didn't strike him as being solvent enough to pay for the plans she'd commissioned, much less the structure she'd asked him to design.

Her plans to destroy prime farm acreage still didn't sit right with him. Russ knew the value of good farmland. He'd expected to own a portion of the family farm one day. But when his parents died in an accident, his brother Wendell received the farm, while he'd received a cash inheritance that enabled him to complete college and live until he established himself in his chosen career.

He supposed that if he'd accepted Wendell's offer to live at the house he could have kept a portion of the funds, but he couldn't stomach the idea of living with the enemy.

Russ often wondered if his decision to become an architect had been the reason his father gave the farm to Wendell. Sure, he loved his work, but he loved Hunter Farm as well. He had seen himself as part of the farm's future, and now Wendell had everything.

He found it impossible to overcome the overwhelming anger toward his brother and parents. Why had he shared that birthright comment with Val Truelove? He never discussed his personal business with clients.

Now she expected him to play a role in destroying yet another farm. What choice did he have? His future rested on his ability to get the job done. No way did he intend to toss more than two years of on-the-job training away over his principles.

Just do the job, Russ, he told himself as he drove toward Lexington.

Two

"Val, phone!" Jules yelled down the hallway.

Drying her hands, she picked up the kitchen extension and called hello.

"Hi. Whatcha doing?"

She recognized Derrick Masters's voice immediately. His continued persistence despite her efforts to discourage him proved disheartening. "Dishes."

"That's no life for a sweet young thing like you. I called to invite you to join me for a little Louisville nightlife. There's a great band playing at this place I know."

"Sorry, Derrick. I'm not into that." She doubted he cared that the only music she truly appreciated was hymns and contemporary Christian songs.

"How do you know if you won't try?" he demanded peevishly.

"I just know."

"Ah, come on, Val. Give a dude a break. Go out with me."

"We've had this discussion before," she said. "I'm not your type."

"You could be if you'd give me a chance."

"It wouldn't work. We want different things out of life. I need to go. Have fun."

He wasn't going to give up, Val thought, a heavy sigh slipping out after she hung up the phone. Derrick had called several times since she'd left her job at Maddy's and even dropped by the farm once. And he'd sent flowers. Each time she'd thanked him and refused his offer of the day.

For years Val had managed to avoid his pursuit, and in turn Derrick had very little use for her until the changes in her financial status made her an acceptable choice. She hoped to meet Mr. Right but knew without a doubt this man was Mr. Wrong.

Walking over to the kitchen door, she looked out onto the star-sprinkled Kentucky sky. The full moon gave the illusion of pale daylight over the expanse of their backyard. She saw her dad sitting alone in the swing. She had sent her parents off to the porch to relax while she tidied the kitchen. After pouring two mugs of coffee, she pushed open the screen door. "Where's Mom?"

"Making sure everyone finished their homework." Jacob Truelove patted the seat. "Come sit with me, my Valentine."

She passed him a mug. "I could have done that."

"You know your mother. She likes to talk with the children before bed."

Val settled at her dad's side, enjoying the comfort she'd always felt in his presence. As the oldest of the children at twenty-seven, she'd sat in this very swing many a night discussing topics too numerous to recall. Jacob Truelove was a good father. He gave freely of his love and taught his children the value of working hard for the things that mattered.

"Thinking about what happened today?" Her father's husky voice filled her ear. "Yes. Praising the Lord and seeking His guidance to keep us on the right path. We took a major step."

One she'd never dreamed of taking. When she'd handed over a check for the down payment on Sheridan Farm, the action had seemed surreal, as if she were dealing with the play money of childhood games and not the real stuff. Val still couldn't believe they owned Sheridan Farm. Sure, she'd fantasized in her youth but found the idea of owning so much now almost frightening.

Even with the down payment they owed a considerable debt. They had debated the wisdom of buying a less expensive acreage;

but Sheridan Farm was home, and the people who worked there were like family. When she'd asked God to provide, she'd had no idea His provision would make them responsible for so much.

Debt had never been part of their lives. Her father's salary and other benefits had enabled their mother to be a stay-at-home mom. She'd budgeted carefully and learned to stretch their money to provide for the needs of their large family. While they might not have had all the things their friends had, they had enough.

The family weighed the pros and cons carefully, and the positives far outweighed the negatives. The well-established horse farm and her father's reputation for producing fine thoroughbreds became number one on the list. Val knew the existing beautiful gardens would save her a fortune when it came to setting up the sites. Knowing there would be an annual income over the years made the decision easier, but they knew the farm needed to cover its operation overhead to be a success. Your Wedding Place would need to do the same.

They had prayed over the situation for several days before making their decision, and as of three o'clock that afternoon her family owned 267 acres of the most beautiful Kentucky bluegrass in Bourbon County. The sale included a more than two-hundred-year-old colonial-style home surrounded by gardens; the manager's home they lived in; tenant houses, horse barns, and paddocks; a number of lakes, creeks, and ponds; a few horses, cows, and other livestock; and so much more.

They had been a quiet group on the drive home. The only celebratory dinner had been the food Opie had waiting on the table. After dinner the younger children had gone off to do their homework, just as they did every other night.

"Regrets?" she asked.

"A finer answer to a prayer has never been received, Valentine."

"But you don't like where the money came from?"

Her father's weathered face changed with his frown. "It's almost poetic justice that my dad gambled away every dime he could get his hands on, and now that same means has provided his heirs with funds to improve the lives of so many."

"Maybe it is," Val agreed. "This money will provide us opportunities we've never imagined."

He took her hand in his. "That's not true, Val. You've had the vision all along. You worked hard to help Rom, Heath, and Opie get a good education. Now is your time."

"They would have taken care of the others, Daddy." She spoke of the plan for the three older siblings to help provide for the educations of their younger sister and brothers.

"Now they can use that knowledge to help with your business."

"Our business," she corrected. "Sheridan Farm and Your Wedding Place are part of Truelove Inc. It's as much yours as mine."

"No, Valentine," he said stubbornly. "The money is yours."

She looked him straight in the eye. "With the exception of the twenty-five acres I plan to use for Your Wedding Place, I'm gifting you and Mom with Sheridan Farm. I trust you to continue doing what you've always done for our family. It's time you worked for yourself. Tell me your dreams for the farm."

"There's only the one, and that's to produce the finest horseflesh Kentucky has ever seen."

Val's laughter blended with the evening sounds and squeak of the chain as it moved against the hooks. "You have plenty of competition, but you've always done the Sheridans proud. I know you'll do the same for the Trueloves."

"Do you think our lives will ever settle down again?"

"I don't know, Daddy. People are already after the money, but it's well invested and protected. I designated funds for the truly needy, but I'm not planning to fulfill any ridiculous requests. We'll be good stewards of what God has provided."

"I've heard some rich people can squeeze a nickel until the buffalo cries out."

"More likely Mr. Lincoln will sing out from my tightwad dealings with his penny."

Her dad chuckled. "God gifted you, Val. You have to make a difference for others as well."

"We will, Daddy. This money isn't going to change us."

"Already we've changed with pride of ownership of Sheridan Farm."

"We've always had pride of accomplishment, Daddy. And I fully attribute our successes to allowing the Lord to direct our paths."

Her father nodded. "Hear from your architect yet?"

Spring might have arrived, but Val could feel a nip in the night air. She rubbed her arms and snuggled closer to her father. She had shared the events of their first meeting with the family over dinner that night. "Not a word. Russell Hunter said his brother owns Hunter Farm just down the road from here."

"I've met Wendell Hunter. The parents died in an accident. Russ must have been the one who was off at college at the time."

"He mentioned his birthright being stolen. Evidently the brother inherited the farm."

"It's sad that two brothers have problems over possessions. What did you really think about him?"

"I'm not sure he's the right man for the job."

"What makes you say that?"

Val knew he'd never let her make an unjustified assumption about anyone. "You should have heard his reaction when I outlined my plans. You'd have thought I was destroying sacred ground."

"You know how some people react to change, Val."

"But it's inevitable. Nothing stays the same. You think it's a good idea, don't you?"

"I can't say I understand why people spend so much money on weddings, but if they're going to do it I see no reason why you shouldn't profit from their choices."

"I prayed about this. When Mr. Sheridan died, I asked God to keep us here if it was

His will. I never expected things would turn out as they have."

"It's a major responsibility. I've never made any secret of how my father's actions hurt him and our family. He allowed his own selfish needs and addictions to take over his life. It was a miserable life, Val. I never wanted that for my children."

"We all know how blessed we are to have you as our father. We love and respect you so much, not only for the sacrifices you've made for us but for the way you prove your love. Quality time is certainly more important than any material possessions. Daddy, do you ever visit Grandfather?"

"Not for some time now. He hasn't changed, Val. He's still about the same as he was before he ended up in prison. Blames everyone but himself; claims he was framed even though there were witnesses."

She looked up at him, much as she'd done since she was a little girl. "But you've forgiven him?"

"I like to think so. Then I have times when I have to seek God's forgiveness for having bad thoughts toward him. My mother destroyed her health because of my father. I find that a very difficult pill to swallow when I read a letter he's written that generally ends in a request for money. I can only imagine what he'll ask for when he hears you've won the money."

"Would you have preferred I didn't accept it?"

He shook his head. "Part of me wanted to tell you to destroy that ticket and let life follow the same path we were on before. But, like you, I believe in the power of prayer, and knowing you earnestly sought and believed God would provide for our future makes me feel it's of God.

"As with everything else you've done in life, I'll stand behind you in this. We'll weather this storm together, and in the end we'll be stronger, better Christians because we trusted God to provide for our needs."

"I love you, Daddy."

"I love you, too, sweetheart. It's getting late. I think I'll go in and read my Bible for a bit before bed."

"Dream bluegrass dreams, Daddy."

He kissed her forehead. "You, too, Valentine."

As she watched her father enter the house, Val thought about the family meeting where she'd made the announcement that changed their lives. Rom and Heath had been home on spring break. Opie arrived just before dinner that night. Every member of the family had been shocked when she told them how she'd come to win several million dollars.

The Hamilton wedding had made for a demanding winter at work. No one had ever been more difficult than the bride who demanded the world with sun, moon, and stars thrown in for good measure. Dealing with divas was part of the job, but Val found the spoiled young woman to be the worst she'd ever experienced in her years at Madelyn Troyer's Wedding Designs. Nothing stood in the way of the woman's plan to have the grandest wedding Lexington society had ever seen. Wendy didn't care whom she stomped on in the process. Val almost felt sorry for the man she was to marry; but then, if possible, she found him even more arrogant than his bride. In the end she decided they made a good couple. At least no one else would have to suffer the extreme boorishness.

The only positive had been that their demands had kept her mind off her own problems. The elder Mr. Sheridan had died, leaving Sheridan Farm to his son, William Sheridan III. The New York lawyer made it clear he did not intend to return to Kentucky.

Val had been almost three when the elder William Sheridan hired her father as his manager. Val, her parents, and the year-old twins, Rom and Heath, had moved into the manager's house on the farm. Before that, they had lived in another tenant house further away. She still remembered her excitement over coming to live with the horses. With the passing of time their family had continued to grow, and all seven of the Truelove children considered Sheridan Farm home. The small town environment of Paris, Kentucky, the thoroughbred capital of the world, fit their family perfectly.

While she knew her dad didn't want to look elsewhere for work, Val accepted it could become reality very soon. Mr. Sheridan had respected her father's beliefs and never forced him to do things that went against his religion. Val feared her father might not find the same sort of atmosphere for future employment. At forty-seven, he had years before retirement.

Val had prayed for an answer, and on Sunday morning the pastor had preached on Matthew 21:22. When he read, "And all things, whatsoever ye shall ask in prayer, believing, ye shall receive," Val had her answer. She had no doubt God would provide, and believed with every bit of her being.

On the Monday following the Hamilton

wedding, Maddy had been all smiles as she passed around lottery tickets. "Thanks for all the hard work you did with the wedding," she said as she handed Val her ticket. "As much as I love my job, there were times when the Hamiltons had me thinking there had to be an easier way to earn a living."

Val fingered the ticket, thinking she would have preferred a cash bonus. She'd come to expect the impractical gifts. Expensive handmade chocolates, massages, and facials weren't bad rewards, but items like wine for a non-drinker and lottery tickets for a non-gambler were a total waste. Not wanting to seem ungrateful, she kept her opinion to herself as she thanked her employer and tucked it in her purse.

A few days later, Val overheard the staff discussing how they were looking for the winner of the biggest Powerball lottery ever. One by one they checked their numbers, groaned their disappointment, and tossed the tickets.

Later, while straightening the area, Val found the abandoned list of winning numbers on the counter. She crumpled the sheet, but curiosity forced her to take a look. She compared the numbers to the ticket from her purse, and in a moment her world changed forever.

Every number was a match. Uncertain what that meant, Val folded the paper and tucked it and the ticket away safely in her purse. After dinner that night she went on the computer and learned she had won millions of dollars.

She'd kept her secret from Thursday to Sunday, seeking guidance from God. Val asked to speak with the pastor privately and explained the situation, asking for his input. She knew her church took a strict stance against gambling and did not accept tithes from such winnings.

"You're innocent in this, but the money does come from gambling proceeds," John David Skipper told her.

"I prayed, Pastor Skipper. I asked God to provide, and I believed He would. How can this be wrong if it's His way of providing?"

"Is it, or do you want it to be?"

Val didn't know what to think. Beyond her prayers and believing God would answer them, she hadn't taken any action to make this happen. She hadn't wasted her precious dollars buying lottery tickets. She'd worked hard and been rewarded with a gift that far exceeded anything she could imagine. "I'm so confused," she admitted. "I don't believe in luck, but I do believe in God's blessings."

"How does your father feel?"

Val sighed. "I haven't told him yet. Daddy's told you about his father?"

The pastor nodded. "You can't keep it from him. You'll need to prepare for the outcome once this becomes public. This much money has a way of bringing out the bad in people."

"I know," Val said.

"But I will say that if anyone is able to handle the situation, I believe your family can. In the time I've had the pleasure of knowing you, I've come to admire the love and dedication you show one another and others. I know you'll use the money to benefit more than your family."

"Thanks, Pastor Skipper. I find it difficult to believe it myself, but I'm convinced God has answered my prayers and His intention is that the money be a blessing. I plan to be a good steward of everything He's entrusted to me."

"I know you mean that, Val, and I will pray for you and the decision."

She left feeling no clearer about what she should do than when she had entered his office. That night at the family meeting Val knew her news troubled her dad.

"All of you know how I feel about gambling," her father said. "It destroyed your grandfather."

"But, Dad," Rom said, "it's an answer to Val's prayer. She believed God would provide and He has."

"Son, the Lord has provided for this family for many years," their dad said.

"All those crazy gifts from your boss, and she finally gives you something that makes you rich," Heath said with a shake of his head. "Have you told her yet?"

"I've only told the family and Pastor Skipper. I went on the computer to see what I needed to do." She explained the process.

"We'll go with you," Rom said.

"Is it okay, Dad?" she asked, looking into doe-brown eyes the same color as her own.

He appeared doubtful. "We need to pray, Val. Make sure this grace is of the Lord. It will change your life."

"Our lives," she countered. "I didn't ask for myself. I asked for all of us. If we take this money, it will be for our family."

"What are your plans?" her mother asked.

She glanced at her dad. "I'll buy Sheridan Farm."

"Are you sure?" he asked.

"Yes, sir. That was my prayer, my belief that God would provide a means for us to stay here — and He has."

Her father frowned. "But with gambling winnings. You know people will believe you bought that ticket."

Val nodded. "I've considered that. But I also know the media will provide me with the opportunity to share the truth."

"Doesn't matter," her father contended. "Those people who want to see it negatively will. Are you prepared to have your coworkers upset because you won what they feel should have been their money? To deal with the demands of complete strangers who feel entitled to share your riches? There are horror stories of people who ended up without a dime to their name after spending their millions. Not to mention those whose lives were destroyed because they did win."

"It won't last," Rom predicted. "People will say, 'Did you hear about the woman in Paris who won all that money?' They'll wish they'd won it, and that will be the end of it."

"I suspect that's wishful thinking on your part, son," her father said. "People with money continually get requests from those who feel entitled. This much money will only serve to make them feel even more so."

"Once they know where Val lives, they'll invade the farm," Heath said.

"We could change to an unlisted number and hire security," she suggested.

Fourteen-year-old Cy spoke up. "I think

35

it's cool."

"You might not think so once your friends treat you differently because you're wealthy," Val warned.

"I'm not wealthy. You are."

"If I am, you are," Val told him.

"Will you buy me a four wheeler?"

"Val won't buy anything that goes against the rules of this family," their father told him.

She smiled at her younger brother. "I'm sure we'll all get things we've dreamed of having, within reason. But we have to bless others as God has blessed us. So, Daddy, what do you think?"

"We should continue to seek the Lord's guidance."

"Mom?"

Cindy Truelove's gaze shifted from her husband back to her oldest daughter. "We trust you to do what's right, Val. God has provided you with a lot of money. It won't be easy."

Her parents' faith in her had gone a long way in reassuring Val. She agreed it wouldn't be an easy task. But as she'd always done in life, she trusted God to lead the way.

Rising from the swing, she went inside and found her sister stretched out on the sofa.

"What are you reading?"

Opie held up one of the free magazines she'd picked up in town. "An article on Paris's most eligible bachelors."

Val laughed. "They actually have some?"

"Yeah, they're having a bachelor auction fund-raiser. Look at this guy," Opie said, pointing to the page. "Wendell Hunter. He believes a woman's sole focus should be her family and home. That's so antediluvian."

"Hunter?" Val shut out Opie's tirade as she reached for the magazine. This was too weird. The Hunter name seemed to turn up with frightening regularity lately. "That's my architect's brother."

"Small world."

Val handed the magazine back, her thoughts on what she'd just read. "How would you like to go to a bachelor auction?"

"Are you nuts?"

Val shrugged. "No. I just thought it might be fun to check out Paris's most eligible bachelors."

"You want to check out your architect's brother."

"I do," she admitted.

"I don't think seeing Wendell Hunter strut the runway is going to give you much insight."

"I don't know. It might tell us more than

you know. I'll buy you a new dress," Val offered. When Opie hesitated, she said, "Shoes, too."

"Okay, I'm in," Opie agreed. "But you have to buy something for yourself as well."

Val should have known the plan would backfire on her. She hated shopping. "Okay. Let's pick Jules up from school and take her and Mom along, too. We could all use some spring clothes."

Opie twisted the top back on the polish bottle and tossed it to her sister. "Do something with those grubby nails."

Val looked at her hands. "They're not that bad. I've been wearing garden gloves."

"If you say so," Opie said, making her examine them more closely. "Are you going into Lexington with us tomorrow?"

Val already had a full schedule for the day. "What's the plan?"

"We're meeting for lunch after Rom's interview. And Heath wants to look into something for Dad's birthday."

"Did he say what he had in mind?"

"The guys have a couple of ideas. Of course, you gave him the best gift today."

Val grinned. "I'd say I'm caught up for years to come."

"Lucky," Opie said.

"Blessed," Val countered. "I'll meet you

guys for lunch. I have an appointment with the English garden first thing tomorrow."

"Want me to stick around and help?"

"Maybe later. Right now I'm hunting for treasure. I pray Rom's interview goes well. It'll be nice to have everyone home again. Have you given more thought to your plans?"

"All the time."

"You'll be around to cook Daddy's birthday supper?"

Opie nodded. "All his favorites. That's my gift."

"Talk about my gift," Val teased. "You truly know the way to his heart. Want to watch television?"

"You think there will be another Val sighting?"

She laughed. The entire family had teased her about interviews she'd given since the win. "I hope not. You think people are getting the message?"

"Definitely. You've given God the glory and talked about being a good steward. In fact, you've handled the publicity as well as any professional. I'm impressed."

"Thanks, Opie. It's pretty nerve-racking, but I believe God is giving me the words."

Her sister grinned at her. "I know. And you're so worn out from writing that big check today that you'll let me control the remote?"

"No way," Val said, settling into the recliner and hitting the ON button. "You make me dizzy with all that channel surfing."

THREE

The moment he spotted Val in her old jeans and grubby UK sweatshirt, Russ knew he should have called first. "Hi. You look busy."

She nodded. "It will take a long time to undo the years of neglect."

"Why not hire someone?"

"I don't mind getting my hands dirty. Besides, the wrong person could do a lot of harm. There's priceless statuary and yard art out here. And I'm trying to restore the Celtic knot garden."

"The Celtic what?"

"It's hard to explain," Val told him. "Mainly it's a very intricate design involving well-pruned boxwood and other plants. I'll show you once it's restored."

Russ nodded and held up the portfolio he carried. "I brought the plans. I hoped you could spare a few minutes."

Stripping off her gloves, she crossed patio stones riddled with grass and weeds. "Bring them over to the table."

Russ avoided the moldy chair cushion and rusted patio table as best he could. He hadn't considered he'd end up wearing his expensive designer suit in the jungle she called a garden. Removing the plan he'd mounted on foam core just before leaving the office, Russ confidently handed it over. He felt rather proud of his work and was eager to hear what Val Truelove had to say. The lengthening silence as she studied the plans made him ask, "Is something wrong?"

"You haven't captured my vision."

Resentment flashed through him at her failure to recognize his hard work. What vision? She wanted a structure in a pasture on a horse farm. What did she think she was going to see? Greek ruins?

"Come with me," she said suddenly, pushing the board in his direction before walking away.

Russ grabbed the plans and scrambled to keep up with her long-legged stride. When Val paused by the oldest, most worn jeep he'd ever seen, he groaned silently.

She climbed inside and started the vehicle on first try. "Get in."

Frowning at the layer of dust coating the interior of the vehicle, Russ pushed the plan board into the back and did as she requested. He hoped Mr. King would find the sacrifice of his favorite suit commendable when it came to satisfying their clients.

"Hold on," Val warned as he looked around for a seat belt that had never existed or long since disappeared from the vehicle.

She drove past outbuildings and fenced areas where men worked the horses that made Sheridan Farm what it should be. She waved at an older man who waved back. "My dad," she volunteered as she stopped the vehicle. "Can you get the gate, please?"

Russ didn't even want to consider what the seat covers were doing to his clothes as he exited the vehicle.

"Make sure it's secure," she called back to him after driving through.

He closed the gate and made his way back to where she waited. A couple of minutes later, Russ grabbed hold of the dashboard when she stopped suddenly, right in the middle of the pasture.

"Can you see it?"

Russ didn't know what she expected him to see. Acres of rolling hills, green with bluegrass and bordered with black fences. A wooded area in the distance. The same place she'd shown him his first day out there. His confusion must have shown.

"What happened to the guy who knew

43

more about Kentucky farmland than anyone else?"

Russ resented her taunting. "I thought I'd designed what you wanted."

"Is it only when horses roam here that you experience the beauty?" she challenged. "Think of it as a balcony overlooking the roaring ocean waves or the vista from a cabin porch overlooking a spectacular range of mountains. What can we do to help them see the magnificence of rolling green hills? How do we make them feel surrounded by something bigger than themselves while celebrating their love with friends and family?"

Russ understood the bigger-than-life part. He'd always felt that when viewing the majestic scenery of the places his parents had taken him when they vacationed. Maybe he had taken home for granted.

Val climbed out of the vehicle and revolved slowly. "I want this structure to be a window to my world. When someone stands here and looks out, I want them to believe there can be no more perfect spot. I want the glorious beauty to push the air from their lungs."

She didn't want much, Russ thought, struggling to determine how he could put her needs on paper.

"Do you understand?"

Her determined expression told him many things about Val Truelove. Quick-minded, sensitive, emotional at times, and temperamental when crossed, she wouldn't make this easy for him. Suddenly it became crucial that he prove he hadn't been blowing smoke when he'd made those claims. "I'll rework the plans. Bring them closer to what you want."

Val came around the vehicle and scrambled in the glove compartment until she found a small digital camera. It took her several minutes to snap the photos of the surrounding area. "Take this with you. Use the photos to give you insight into what suits the area."

He should have thought of that. "Thanks," he said, sliding the camera into the interior pocket of his suit.

On the drive back Russ asked, "Have you contacted the zoning department about your proposed changes?"

He could tell from her frown that he'd reminded her of his comment on their first meeting.

"My lawyer is looking into the requirements," Val said. "I suppose we're already zoned for business because of the horse farm."

"You're zoned for a horse farm. If you plan to convert the house to a bed-and-breakfast, there will be stipulations for parking and handicap access, and interior changes to meet code requirements. Since I don't even know how they'll categorize your business, they'll probably need a detailed business plan. Have you attended a chamber meeting yet? You should. Get word out about your intentions."

"Sounds complicated."

"It could be. Have you developed the business plan?"

"No more than I showed you when we first started talking. I can expand. Show how much money couples spend annually on weddings and venues. I'm sure Maddy has data she would share."

"I'd contact the city first," Russ suggested. "Then provide the information they request. What sort of time frame are you looking at on the structure?"

"I'd love to have it completed by my mom's birthday in early November. We're planning a combination party and family reunion."

"I doubt it'll be done by then."

"I'll have to make alternate arrangements. Opie's planning the menu while I procure the location."

"Opie?"

"My sister."

"So you have a sister?"

"Actually I have two sisters and four brothers."

He'd had no idea there were so many Truelove kids. Despite his claim of having lived on a horse farm, Russ had spent very little time at Hunter Farm. When he became old enough, his father shipped him off to boarding school and then he'd traveled abroad with his mother in the summer.

They negotiated the rest of the trip in silence, and once she parked at the house he climbed out of the vehicle, forcing back the desire to brush the dust off his suit. He didn't want to offend Val Truelove again. "I'll get back to you next week."

Russ had no idea what he'd have to offer. Right now he was drawing a complete blank.

"This isn't for me," Val said. "I want this for my clients. I already know what a treasure we have in Kentucky."

Two hours later his coworker and fellow architect, Kelly Dickerson, glanced up when Russ walked into the office. "How did it go this morning?"

He had stopped by the drugstore to print the pictures Val had taken, hoping to find something that would inspire him to the heights she expected.

"I should have made an appointment. She was working in the garden and after looking at my plans insisted we ride out to the site in what must have been one of the first jeeps ever made. I'll probably never get my suit clean."

Kelly flashed him a sympathetic smile. "She didn't like your plans?"

Fresh irritation surged through Russ. "Said I didn't see her vision. Spouted some nonsense about a window to the world." He held up the packet of photos. "I hope these help me get a visual. I'm certainly not seeing anything at present."

Kelly rolled her chair back. "Spread them out. Let's take a look."

As he laid the 8 × 10 glossies around on the drawing board, Russ noted each picture seemed to represent a different angle of the area she planned to convert. He rearranged a couple of prints and glanced at Kelly. "See anything?"

"Tell me what she said."

He attempted to recall Val Truelove's exact words.

Kelly nodded. "She's right, you know. Either you make the structure stand out, or you choose the most breathtaking vista. The perfect design would be a combination of

the two. Look at how she shot the photos,"
she said, tapping a scene of a pasture filled
with gorgeous thoroughbred horses. "Where
would you stand to see this? Would there be
only one lookout point from the structure?
If not, what could you do to make every
scene breathtaking? Would you want this as
a backdrop to your event?"

Russ threw his hands up in the air. "You've
got me."

"Maybe it's a woman thing," Kelly said
finally. "I think I understand what she's trying to help you see."

"Then let me in on the secret," Russ
requested earnestly. He'd never felt so at
odds with a project.

She shrugged. "I'd only be guessing.
You're the one who talked to Val. She told
you what she wanted. Just remember —
beauty is in the eye of the beholder. Look at
these and decide what you think is beautiful. Let's hope you'll hit on the same things
she's seeing."

Kelly went back to her drawing board, and
Russ continued to study the pictures. "She
has two sisters and four brothers," he commented idly. "What I don't understand is
how they can afford this. I'm sure she paid
a fortune for the farm and is now making
long-range plans for a business that may or

may not prove profitable. Where did she get her money?"

"Honestly, Russ, don't you ever watch the news?" his coworker asked. "Your client won one of the biggest Powerball lotteries ever."

His mouth fell open. "You're kidding. She said her ship came in."

"I'd say the fleet," Kelly said with a laugh. "She can certainly afford any vision she wants."

"But . . . ," Russ stammered. "You should see her."

"I know Val from church," Kelly said. "The Trueloves are a nice family. They are a very driven group. Believe in helping each other. Rumor has it Val spent nearly every dime of her earnings on Rom's, Heath's, and Opie's education. Of course they're very intelligent and had scholarships as well. The twins were the first co-valedictorians at our school."

"I don't get it," Russ said. "If she's rich, why is she doing this?"

"I think you'll find the Trueloves are a unique family," Kelly told him. "I've worked with them on church projects, and they don't do anything by half."

"I can believe that," Russ agreed, his gaze moving to the pictures that represented

Kentucky through Val Truelove's eyes. "Guess I'd better get to work."

"Just focus on what you saw, Russ," Kelly advised. "And what Val said. She has a vision, and it's your job to get it on paper. I doubt she will accept anything less than perfection."

The work took on a more personal aspect for Russ, and he found himself struggling to design something that would please Val. The need to prove his ability was stronger than ever after the morning's meeting.

"When does Val plan to start booking?" Kelly asked.

Russ hesitated. Val had been adamant about keeping the plans a secret. "She's working in the gardens now. Why?"

"Gabe and I are still looking for a wedding site."

"I thought you'd decided on the church."

"We go back and forth. I'd love an outdoor wedding."

"So what's wrong with your mom's garden?"

"It's not big enough. We need seating for at least two hundred. Do you think she'd book my wedding? I've heard the Sheridan Farm gardens are incredible."

Even in their overgrown state Russ had seen their potential. He dug through the papers on his desk and found the card Val had given him. "There's only one way to find out. Give her a call."

"I will. Maybe it's a woman thing, but I saw something very appealing in those pictures."

"Mr. King should have assigned the job to you."

"No, thanks. I have as much as I can handle with planning a wedding."

"How about I put the pictures on the wall and you share your thoughts?"

"I already do that, Russ."

"I'm really floundering on this one, Kel. I didn't make a good first impression."

"Oh, Russ, what did you say?"

"Mostly comments about how she didn't know what it meant to live on a horse farm and I did."

When Kelly burst out laughing, Russ demanded, "What's so funny?"

"Jacob Truelove has managed the Sheridan property since Val was a toddler. She's spent her life around horses."

It bothered him that he'd been denied an opportunity to live on the farm. Russ drew a deep breath and closed his eyes. "When will I ever learn to keep my opinion to myself?"

"Probably never."

"She must have found my ignorance entertaining."

"Don't mess this up, Russ," Kelly warned. "You've invested too much time at Prestige Designs."

"I'll see her vision or die trying."

"That's the spirit," Kelly encouraged. She glanced at her watch. "I have a lunch meeting with Mr. King and a client."

"That's right. Go enjoy yourself while I attempt to read Val Truelove's mind."

"I don't think she's looking for a psychic," Kelly said with a big grin.

"I think that's exactly what she wants. A psychic in a handsome young architect's body."

"Oh, spare me, please," Kelly said with a loud guffaw as Randall King opened the door.

"Ready, Kelly?"

They looked up guiltily.

"Yes, sir. I'll meet you out front."

Their boss didn't seem in a hurry to depart. "How's your project going, Russ?"

"I'm refining my ideas."

"Hated them, didn't she?" Mr. King asked, his knowing smirk irritating Russ even more.

"She has a vision, but I haven't given up."

"Remember, it's your job to guide her.

People don't always know what they want."

Russ didn't feel that was true when it came to Val. She knew exactly what she wanted. "I'll keep you informed."

"I'll make sure you do."

Russ watched Randall King stroll out the door, reluctantly admiring the man's confident swagger. One day he would have his own office and be the one issuing orders rather than taking them. He forced himself to concentrate on the photos. Val's enthusiasm when she talked about showing the world the greater picture forced Russ to ask himself how to do that.

In his mind he saw the pastoral peacefulness of rolling hills and beautiful horses grazing on rich green grass within miles of meandering black fences. "What else?" he asked, finding it difficult to put himself on a mountaintop in the middle of a pasture. Or was it? He paused from shuffling the photos. What if the structure floor became her balcony? The acres of bluegrass her ocean?

As the idea took hold Russ hurried over to his computer, eager to capture this thought.

FOUR

After Russ left and she'd returned to the garden, all Val could think about was the plans he had presented. They had been substandard to say the least. Did he honestly believe he'd given her what she wanted?

Russ Hunter hadn't liked that she'd kept him in the garden either, but she'd been grimy from working outside and hadn't particularly wanted to take the dirt into the grand room Mr. Sheridan had called his office.

Why hadn't he seen her vision? Every great view was an overlook to the world. Granted, Paris, Kentucky, wasn't the world, but she considered it as beautiful as those other places. Val couldn't imagine anything more spectacular than the view the wedding guests would see from the structure.

Disappointment stabbed at her. She'd considered him rather handsome when she welcomed him into the office, but his arrogance had made a bad impression. Val thought of how he'd changed after she'd all but thrown him out. He'd shoveled on the charm. Because she wanted her project underway she'd given him another chance. He'd forced her to do the same again today. How many opportunities did Mr. Hunter think she'd give him?

The way he'd acted when she chose to drive the old jeep to the site had been almost entertaining. He'd tried unsuccessfully to disguise his dismay. She figured a dry cleaning bill would show up on her account but didn't care. If it helped him design what she wanted, she'd pay for a new suit. Val knew she shouldn't have done that, but deep down inside she believed him more competent than she'd witnessed today. She'd hired a professional, but what she'd gotten was little better than her own amateurish efforts.

"Did I do the right thing, Lord?" she asked. That same question came to mind several times daily as Val struggled with the decision she'd made. Accepting the money had enabled her to help her family in ways she'd never imagined, but at what cost? Would she come to regret what she'd done? "Guide me. Show me what You would have me do with the money and the plans You have for our family."

They already had everything they needed. Sheridan Farm had supported their family for years, and Val knew her father would do everything possible to ensure it continued to do so. But there was no role for her. She didn't want to raise horses or do farm chores.

"If this is Your will, dear Lord, help Russ create the plans that will make this work. Guide his hand in the drawing and help me find contentment in the idea."

She snipped at the vine wrapped around the statuary. Pulling the angel free, she set it over to the side. Val knew she had given God complete control and listened when He told her what to do. Everything would be okay. She believed that with every breath in her body. God's peace enveloped her there in the gardens.

Val loaded another wheelbarrow with debris. Why had Mr. Sheridan allowed everything to get so out of control? Surely he'd seen it every time he visited the gardens. Then again maybe he hadn't come out here much after his wife's death. Hadn't Daddy spoken of how heartbroken the old man had been after the loss of his wife of more than fifty years? The thought saddened Val.

Glancing at her watch, she quickly picked up her tools and headed for the house to shower and dress for the trip into Lexington. Standing beneath the spray of hot water, her conscience pricked at the way she'd treated Russ. She had been rough on him. It was possible she hadn't made herself clear. Still, anyone could have provided something that basic.

She found his boyish charm and chiseled jaw appealing and wanted to tousle his neatly styled thick brown hair. The penetrating stare of those blue eyes had a powerful effect as well.

It was nearly twelve thirty when she slipped into the booth where Opie waited. "Where's Heath?"

"He's on his way. Did you get a lot done this morning?"

"No," Val said after requesting a glass of ice water with lemon. "Russ Hunter showed up with the most pitiful set of plans I've ever seen. I drove him and his fancy suit to the site in the jeep."

Opie gasped. "You didn't."

Val nodded. "I sent him off with an earful of what I expected when he comes back."

"How did he react?"

"Surprised. I think he expected me to love what he'd done. For all his big talk I expected better. I hope he's not letting his attitude affect his work."

"You think he's trying to sabotage your idea?"

Val shrugged. "That doesn't make sense. He's paid when I'm satisfied with his work. Seems to me that jeopardizing my project would do him more harm than it would me."

"True," Opie agreed. "There's Heath." She waved at him.

Their brother slipped into the opposite side of the booth. "No word from Rom?" When Opie shook her head, he said, "His interview must have lasted longer than he thought."

"That could be a good thing," Opie said.

"Let's hope so," Val agreed.

"Did you find them?" Opie asked Heath.

"No. I found a source. I can order and have them here in plenty of time."

"What are you looking for?" Val asked curiously.

"Rom and I thought new horse blankets bearing Daddy's name would be a great birthday gift. We need someone to design a new logo."

A doodler by nature, Val had twined a T with a heart and a horse's head into the logo she used on the Truelove Inc. business cards. Pulling one from her purse, she asked, "What about this?"

"Your work?" When she nodded, Heath said, "Looks great. More creative than anything I came up with."

"What color? Royal blue?" All the kids knew that was their dad's favorite color.

Heath nodded. "With gold lettering and trim."

"He'll love them. He was just saying the other day that some of the old Sheridan blankets have seen better days."

"Val was telling me about the plans Russ Hunter brought by this morning," Opie said.

Heath glanced at his older sister. "Good?"

Val shook her head. "Pitiful."

"She took Mr. Hunter for a ride in the jeep," Opie said.

"You didn't." Heath's disbelief echoed Opie's.

Val shrugged. "It's the easiest way to get there."

"You could have used a nicer vehicle," Opie said.

"He irritated me," Val admitted. "Showed up without an appointment, wearing a suit that cost more than I made in months, acting pleased as punch with himself over a set of substandard plans."

"That's not very Christian."

"I know." Her voice rose. "He pushes my buttons and then piles on the charm. You should have heard him go on that first meeting about how he had a right to be concerned about my plans for the farm."

"Maybe you should get another architect," Heath suggested.

"I'll give him one more chance," Val said. "If this next set of plans isn't what I expect, I'm calling Randall King."

"I could deal with Russ Hunter for you," Heath offered.

Val smiled at her brother. "Thanks, but no. If I'm going to be in business, I need to learn to deal with all kinds of people."

"Especially handsome young architects that get under her skin," Opie said with a giggle. Heath laughed, and Val couldn't help but join in.

They hushed when another patron approached the small table across from their booth. Val immediately recognized the young woman. "Jane, hi," she called. "How's the job hunt going?"

Jane took a step closer to the booth. "Not so good."

Val glanced at Heath. "You remember Jane Kendrick from school?"

Heath looked startled but quickly regained

his composure. "Sure do. It's good to see you."

Jane flashed him a wide grin. "You, too. Val keeps me current. Congratulations on your degree. How's Rom?"

"Thanks. He's good. We're waiting on him now. He had an interview today."

"Hope his luck is better than mine," Jane said. "I should have accepted that clerk position."

"No, you shouldn't have," Val protested. She and Jane had become friends when she used to visit the coffee shop during her workdays in Lexington. "I have a couple of ideas that might work for you in the future."

"Now is my future," Jane said unhappily. "I have to find work."

"You will. Join us for lunch."

"Yes, please do," Opie added.

"I don't want to intrude."

"You know us Trueloves. The more the merrier," Opie said.

Jane agreed and asked for a diet soda.

"Why don't you come out to the farm tomorrow? I have an idea I'd like to discuss with you."

"Can I bring Sammy? I called in the last of my favors for the interview today."

"Please do. Daddy might even take her for a ride."

"She'd love that. She's so horse crazy right now."

"Who's Sammy?" Heath asked.

"My two-year-old."

"You have a daughter?" When Jane nodded, Heath said, "I know Garrett is very happy."

Jane paled. "Garrett's dead, Heath."

"Oh, man, I'm sorry. I didn't know. What happened?"

Val and Opie shook their heads in warning, but it was too late.

"He killed himself," Jane said, her voice breaking.

Opie noted Heath's stunned expression and interceded. "Wouldn't you love to see a picture of Jane's daughter, Heath?"

He jumped, and Val knew Opie had kicked him under the table. She hid her smile.

He recovered quickly. "Sure. Is she as pretty as her mom?"

Val noticed the blush that touched the woman's cheeks.

"She's beautiful," Jane declared, digging out her photos. "But that's a very prejudiced mom talking."

As they oohed and aahed over Sammy, Val glanced up and saw Russ walking across the room.

"Don't look now," she whispered to Opie,

"but that's Russell Hunter."

Opie looked up.

"I said don't look," Val hissed just as he approached their table. Recovering her poise, she said, "Russ, I didn't think I'd see you again today."

"Me either. I just wanted to let you know I've been hard at work since I left the farm this morning. I think I might be headed in the right direction this time."

"That's good news. Let me introduce you to everyone. This is my sister, Ophelia," she said with a pointed look.

Opie held out her hand. "Pleased to meet you. Call me Opie. Everyone else does."

"Our friend Jane Holt. My brother Heath."

"My pleasure," Russ said.

When he reached to shake Heath and Jane's hands, Opie leaned over to Val and whispered, "Good thing he didn't mess up the suit. He looks like a million dollars."

When Val attempted to elbow her, Opie moved out of the way and asked, "Are you here for lunch?" When Russ nodded, she invited him to join them. "Valentine," she began, throwing down the gauntlet by sharing Val's real name, "has been telling us about your plans."

"Really?" Russ asked, glancing at Val.

"She said you're reworking them."

He deflated a little. "I think I have a better understanding of what she wants."

"You have to stay," Opie insisted. "We'd love to hear what you think."

"You have a full table."

"We need to ask for a larger one anyway," Opie said. "Our brother Rom should be here any minute. I'm sure he'd love to meet you."

Russ glanced at Val. "Do you mind?"

"Not at all."

Heath signaled their waiter, and Val grabbed Opie's arm when they started to move. "I owe you one."

Opie grinned at Val's promise of payback. "Not with some of the stunts you've pulled. Come on before Heath puts his foot in it again with Jane."

Val followed, not caring for the way this luncheon was going. She hadn't planned to spend any more time in Russ Hunter's company that day.

After being seated, Russ said, "All of you have nicknames."

"We prefer them to our real names. Mom loves the classics. Daddy said she read a lot when she was expecting so I think she chose her favorite name at the time. I'm Valentine. Heath is Heathcliff. Rom is Romeo. Opie is

65

Ophelia. There's a Juliet, Rochester and Darcy at home."

"That's Jules, Roc and Cy," Opie threw out with a grin.

"Valentine?" he asked with a raised brow. "What classic did your mom find that in?"

"I was born on February 14. A little too obvious, don't you think?"

"You could have been Cupid."

"Val works fine, thank you."

"Did you get teased about your names?"

"Some, but eventually everyone started using nicknames like we did."

"We're happy Mom didn't let Daddy name us," Opie said. "Somehow Truelove's Fancy just doesn't do it for me."

Their laughter filled the small room. Rom arrived, and there were more greetings and introductions before they got around to placing their orders.

"I hear you had an interview this morning," Russ said to Rom.

He named the prestigious Lexington company. "I hope to get into their leadership rotational program."

"How do you think it went?" Val asked.

"Pretty good. They're going to get back to me by the end of the week."

"Is it what you want?" Val asked.

"Let's discuss it later," Rom said. "So,

66

Russ, tell me about these plans for Val's business."

Russ admitted he was still trying to figure out exactly what Val wanted.

"Good luck," Rom said. "Val always knows what she wants but leaves it to the rest of us to figure out on our own."

"I do not."

"I hope to be on the same wavelength with the next set of plans," Russ said.

"Val won't settle for anything but the best," Opie warned. "This is important to her."

"I know," Russ said. "I'm trying to wrap my mind around majestic vistas."

Everyone offered their opinion of what that meant, and the conversation moved on to other topics. Russ glanced at his watch. "I'd better get back to the office. I've enjoyed meeting all of you."

"You, too," Opie said. "Feel free to visit the farm anytime."

"Lunch is on me," Russ said. "I'll be in touch soon, Val."

"Wow," Opie said after he walked away. "He's cute."

"Knock it off," Val said, not wanting her sister to find Russ Hunter attractive.

"I need to go, too," Jane said, pushing her

chair back. "It's been great seeing everyone again."

"Please come to the farm tomorrow," Val said. "I really want to talk to you."

"Sure," Jane said. "Just name a time. I have a serious gaping hole in my schedule at present."

"Come around eleven and stay for lunch."

"You don't have to keep feeding me," Jane protested with a smile.

Val thought the young woman had lost too much weight in the months since her husband's death.

"I'll make one of my culinary specialties," Opie said.

"We'll be there," she said. "I warn you Sammy's a picky eater."

"She's never had an Opie Truelove meal."

"Is that like a fast-food kid's meal?" Val teased.

"Once she tastes my food, you'll have problems getting her to eat anything else."

Jane laughed. "I'll risk it. Thanks for lunch."

"Don't thank us," Val said. "Russ Hunter paid."

"Thank him for me next time you see him."

Val nodded, wondering if the meal would show up on her expense report as she made a mental note to thank him for everyone.

"How's it going?" Kelly asked when she returned later that afternoon.

"I have an idea or two. How was your meeting?"

"The client approved the plans and is going to talk with Kevin Flint. Mr. King's happy about that."

Russ laid down his pencil and flexed his shoulders. "What do you suppose he meant by that comment about Val Truelove hating the plans? How did he know?"

Kelly hung her suit coat over the back of her chair and sat down. "Your body language. Usually you're more confident with your successes."

"I wondered if he'd looked at my concept before I presented it to her."

"I think it was because you didn't exude your usual cockiness."

"I'm not like that."

"Sure you are. Stop worrying. You're sounding paranoid."

He was, Russ realized. "It struck me as strange. I thought maybe she'd complained."

"Did she indicate she planned to do that?"

"No, but if he called to follow up, she might have said something."

"I doubt he did that. Maybe if they were friends or ran into each other on the street."

As far as Russ knew, Val and Randall King had never met. She had spoken to him on the phone when she called Prestige looking for an architect. "She didn't mention talking to him at lunch."

That caught Kelly's attention. "You had lunch with her?"

Russ nodded. "And her sister, two brothers, and a friend of theirs."

"Any leads come out of the conversation?"

"Her brother says she always knows what she wants and leaves it to them to figure out on their own."

"That sounds like something a brother would say."

"Or a man would think," Russ said. "I believe most women operate that way."

"Hey," Kelly said with a laugh. "For the record, men are just as confusing as women."

"I enjoyed meeting them," Russ admitted.

"I told you. The Trueloves are nice people."

"At least I have to plan a structure to please only one of them."

"I'm sure they will want a family meeting once the plan is completed," Kelly warned.

"All of them?"

"All of them," Kelly agreed with a nod.

FIVE

Though she hadn't intended to talk to Russ Hunter until he presented the revised plans, Val was forced to call him the following Monday. "Kelly Dickerson called. I thought we agreed my plans would remain confidential."

"We work in the same office," he explained. "She's been looking for a place for a while now. She seemed excited by the idea of getting married at Sheridan Farm."

"She's coming out to take a look at the gardens this weekend. We'll discuss the details then. Meanwhile, I suggest you make her aware this isn't something I want discussed."

"I will," Russ said quickly. "I should have called you myself. I had the photos spread over my drawing board, and she offered a future bride's point of view."

"Did it help?"

"Some. I'm making progress. Did you apply for your business license?"

"It's in the works."

"Is it safe to start booking now?" Russ asked. "What happens if things don't work out?"

"If we come to an agreement, Kelly will have her wedding regardless of the outcome. Sheridan Farm belongs to our family, and as far as I'm aware no laws prohibit an owner from having a wedding at their home."

"What about the business plan?"

"Rom and Heath are looking it over. And I downloaded the information on converting the house to a bed-and-breakfast."

"It doesn't seem right. Houses like that deserve to be loved by their owners," Russ said. "The Sheridan family loved and lived in that home for over two hundred years. Why don't you live there?"

"Alone?"

"I'm sure the family would agree if you suggested you live there."

"I think you give me far more credit than I deserve," Val said.

"Wouldn't you love to call the Sheridan mansion home?"

Though she hadn't admitted it to anyone, Val had been disappointed when her parents refused to leave the manager's house. She and Russ agreed in one regard. It was a shame to leave such a beautiful home unoccupied. "We'll see," she said. "It would have to be occupied if we turn it into a B and B."

"Why are you doing this?" Russ asked.

"I told you. It's a longtime dream."

"But you're rich. You can afford other dreams. Bigger, better ones."

He knew. Val sighed. She'd wondered how long it would be before he heard about the money. "I've always been rich, blessed with hardworking parents who loved me."

"You won the lottery. That's wild."

"The decision over whether or not to keep the money has been a struggle. Daddy's very antigambling. In fact, all of us are."

"But he allowed you to buy the farm with lottery winnings?"

"The ticket was a gift from my employer."

"Dress it up however you want, but it's still lottery winnings."

Why did everyone insist on making her feel she'd done something wrong? "That made the decision difficult."

"How can claiming millions of dollars be difficult?"

"It's a responsibility with a heavy price tag. If I'd gone out and purchased the ticket, it would be different."

"Sounds like you're trying to justify something you don't feel right about."

He hit the bull's-eye with that one. Val's sigh reached over the miles. "Daddy is afraid people will judge me harshly for the choice I made. The Sheridans' son wasn't interested in holding on to the farm. I couldn't bear the thought of giving up the only home most of us kids can remember and Daddy having to seek employment elsewhere. What would you have done? Would you have turned the money down?"

"No."

She knew from his quick response that Russ didn't understand her reaction. "I couldn't either. All I know is that I believed God would provide. It happened in a way I don't really understand. Maddy gave me a gift that made me wealthy."

"I don't get it. Why do you care?"

"Because it's not how we operate. Daddy's father gambled and drank away every penny he could get his hands on. He killed a man and ended up in prison when Daddy was seventeen years old. My father learned his work ethic from an overworked, underpaid mother.

"He worked two and three jobs to support his family and help his brother through college. My grandmother worked for the

Sheridans for a while and got Daddy his first job on the horse farm. He learned everything he could, and when the Sheridans' old manager retired, Mr. Sheridan considered him ready to take on the job. Nothing has ever been easy for him."

"But that's changed now."

"Not really. Daddy will always work hard. He expects us to do the same. No matter what people think, life is not a free ride. We are our brother's keeper."

Russ frowned. His brother could keep himself. He didn't owe Wendell the time of day. Not after the way he had looked out for himself. Older by five years, Wendell had done everything to avoid his pesky half brother. Even at school, Wendell made it clear that Russ should keep his distance. After college, Wendell returned home to the family farm, and Russ had no doubt he'd spent the intervening years ingratiating himself with their father.

"I still don't get the lottery part. Why sweat what people say?"

"Dad says we have to use the money to improve other people's lives as well as our own."

"Pass it on, only on a grander scale?"

"Not grander. It's hard, Russ. We're setting up the rules as we go, but we're trying to make a difference. When I asked God to provide, I had no idea it would be this spectacular. I did believe He would answer my prayer. I figured the new owner would see Daddy's worth and allow him to work out his remaining years here at the farm while we made sure the younger kids were educated as well.

"That's a Truelove tradition. Daddy helped pay for his brother's education, and in turn Uncle Zeb helped Aunt Karen. He's a professor at Harvard. Aunt Karen is a scientist involved in cancer research. The twins just received their MBAs from Harvard, and Opie graduated from culinary school."

"So the oldest kids always lose in the Truelove tradition?"

"I derived a great deal of personal satisfaction from making a difference in their lives. Uncle Zeb and Aunt Karen helped, too."

"Your father helped them, and they helped his kids in return?"

"Rom, Heath, and Opie would have helped our younger siblings."

"But now you'll take care of them as well?"

"Some of the money has been earmarked for an education fund, and we're considering expanding beyond family needs."

"So what do your relatives think about

the win?"

"They agree I was blessed. I actually considered the ticket a waste of good money when Maddy handed it to me."

"I imagine she wishes she had kept it for herself."

"She hasn't said. I owe her and feel we can work together on this venture. Please, Russ, don't discuss this project with anyone else. Ask Kelly to do the same. I don't want a lot of headaches because someone takes exception at this stage."

"It's difficult not to bounce ideas off each other when you share an office."

"I know, but there's so much to finalize before I go public."

"I'll talk to Kelly. And I'll keep your plans so under wraps you'll have to pry them out of me."

She chuckled. "You've got the right idea, but let's not go that far."

Russ Hunter was going to be trouble, Val thought as she laid the cordless phone on the desk. She'd asked him to keep the plans confidential, and yet his office mate had a very good working knowledge of what she intended here at Sheridan Farm.

Val didn't like that. If she'd wanted anyone apprised of her plans, she would be the one doing the informing. She planned to make doubly certain Kelly understood the need for secrecy when she saw her this weekend. Any misinformation at this point could cause major problems.

She picked up the phone again and dialed her lawyer's office. "Mr. Henderson, please. This is Val Truelove calling."

In a few moments the man who had taken on the job of counsel for Truelove Inc. asked, "What can I do for you today, Ms. Truelove?"

"I need to know how I can protect my idea for Your Wedding Place."

"It's an expensive undertaking that will prohibit a number of people from considering the idea. I suppose you could franchise. Do you feel that once the basic premise is established, others would see the merit and develop similar concepts in different locations?"

"I don't know. My plan is to focus my investment on Your Wedding Place. I have no plans to expand beyond Kentucky."

"Franchising is not cheap, but it could be a way to protect your idea. Let me do more research and get back to you."

What was it with everyone? Val thought as she agreed and said good-bye. She was ready to get started while everyone else seemed equally determined to delay the process. "Oh, well, back to the garden," she said, pushing herself out of the executive chair.

"Where's Jane?" Val asked when she found Heath working alone.

"She went into Paris for those plants you wanted."

Val nodded. She had to hand it to the woman. Ever since Jane had accepted the job as her assistant, she'd taken on every task without complaint.

She picked up a pair of gardening gloves and pulled them on. "I wish I'd invited Jane to go to the bachelor auction with us. It was fun."

"What possessed you to bid on that date with Wendell Hunter for Opie?"

"She was interested," Val said, feeling guilty about the prank. She didn't know what got into her when she took Opie's paddle and bid until she won.

"Opie says she's not going."

"She'll go," Val said with surety. "She's dying to tell Wendell Hunter what she thinks of his saying a woman's place is in the home. I just provided the opportunity."

"Well, leave Jane out of it," Heath warned. "She's got enough issues."

She stopped sorting through the tools and looked at Heath. "What do you mean?"

"She's angry at Garrett."

"I'd be angry, too."

"She has to forgive him if she ever hopes to move on with her life."

"That's easier said than done."

Heath sighed. "I know. I hate that she's attempting to deal with this alone. She needs God in her corner."

"I asked if we could take Sammy to church with us on Sunday, and she agreed."

"What about Jane?" he asked.

"Not yet, but I plan to keep inviting her. They're moving into the apartment this weekend. I told her we'd help if she needs us."

"I'm sure she'll try to do it on her own," Heath said.

Val nodded. Jane was having problems accepting their generosity. When she'd shared that her landlord had sold the house she rented, Val offered the two-bedroom efficiency over the garage as part of her salary package. Jane resisted at first but accepted after Val pointed out that they housed a number of the staff at the farm. "Maybe she'll accept our help. She's coming around. Said the apartment is one of the best perks she's ever had."

"Makes sense," Heath said. "With the price of gas she'll save a bundle." He reached for the hedge trimmer. "We're wasting daylight."

The heat of the day seemed to intensify as they trimmed the tall hedges. Within an hour, Val's arms ached from holding them over her head. As lunchtime approached, all she wanted to think about was a cold shower and a nap.

"Hello, stranger."

Startled, Val turned to find Derrick Masters standing nearby. She turned off the trimmer.

"I was in the neighborhood and thought I'd stop by for a visit since you're too busy for your old friends," he said, flashing a big smile.

When had they ever been friends? Derrick hadn't had the time of day for her before the win. "As you can see there's plenty to do. Feel free to jump in."

"I would, but I have plans."

"I understand completely." Val hid her grin. Derrick was allergic to real work.

"Maybe some other time," he suggested. "You still haven't taken me up on my offer to enjoy a bit of Louisville nightlife."

"I'm not the least interested in partying, Derrick. You know that."

"Dinner then. The two of us. A nice restaurant. Candles. A little wine."

Unimpressed by his attempt at romance, Val asked bluntly, "What purpose would it serve?"

"We could get to know each other better."

"You're welcome to join us for dinner here."

"I want to spend time with you," he whined. "I don't do the family thing."

"God and my family are the most important aspects of my life," Val said.

Exasperated, Derrick snapped, "I don't get you. There are lots of women who'd jump at the opportunity to go out with me."

Heath stepped around the hedge. "Then why don't you go find one of them?" His voice lacked his usual friendliness.

"Who are you?"

Heath took a step forward. Derrick took a step back. Her brothers might not be big men, but they had a presence about them when the situation warranted. "Heath Truelove. Val's brother. I'd be happy to introduce you to my twin and our father if you need further convincing."

"It's her loss," Derrick said.

"A decent man would have a true jewel in my sister, and I'm not talking dollars and cents," Heath said, leaving very little doubt about his opinion of the man.

"You Trueloves are crazy." Derrick flung

the words at them before stomping off to his car.

"Thanks," Val said.

"Let me know if he bothers you again."

"You can't always protect me," Val said.

"Sure I can. That's what brothers are for."

"It's not your battle."

"This isn't the first time he's called since you won the money, is it?"

"No. He's determined to take me to Louisville to party."

Heath frowned. "Why isn't he getting the message?"

"Derrick's ego gets in the way of his seeing the truth. He thinks women should feel privileged to be in his presence. I saw through him from day one, but he had a reputation to uphold. When I rejected him, he tried to make me look bad. Evidently the money renewed his interest."

"Men like that give the rest of us a bad name."

"You frightened him. He wasn't expecting you to show up."

"Then maybe we've seen the last of him. Ready to get back to work?"

Val looked up at the tall wall of shrubbery and asked wearily, "Do we have to?"

Heath shrugged. "Only if you hope to finish these gardens anytime soon."

"Can we at least take a water break? I'm parched."

"Go ahead. I'll finish up here."

Val reached for the hedge trimmer. "If you work, I work."

Six

Kelly Dickerson had booked her August wedding. Val was thrilled with her first success, but she also worried things were moving too fast. Suddenly the possibility had become reality, and she wasn't sure they'd be ready.

The idea she needed to make more people aware of her plans wouldn't go away. In a way, that knowledge could be her defense. If more people knew about Your Wedding Place, it would help her defend herself against anyone trying to steal her idea. In the same vein, it could cause the problems she wanted to avoid.

After discussing it with the family over breakfast, she resolved to make an appointment with her former employer. She wanted to hear what Maddy thought about their working together. Heath and Rom had left for Boston the previous Sunday afternoon, and Jane was running errands, so Val headed to the office to make her call.

She knew something was up when her dad came in a few minutes later, his body tense with anger and a frown on his face. "Your grandfather knows about the money."

Her grandfather's calls always disturbed her dad, but today seemed worse than usual. "Did he mention it specifically?"

"He asked why none of his grandchildren ever came to visit him. Particularly his favorite, Val."

"Favorite?" she repeated, her laughter was tinged with disbelief. "I've seen him maybe twice in my life. He doesn't even know me."

"I don't want you giving him money. Karen, Zeb, and I give him sufficient to meet his needs."

"I don't mind, Daddy."

"I do," he declared angrily. "I won't have him taking advantage of you. He'll bleed you dry and step over the body without remorse. I couldn't stop my mother, but I can forbid you. I knew this would happen the moment he learned you'd won that money. Why are people so greedy? I'd rather live out my days as a poor man than be that way."

Val found the pain in his eyes heartbreaking. She'd never seen this side of her father. "Does he know you own Sheridan Farm?"

"No. Zeb, Karen, and I agreed a long time ago to keep our business private. He's a user, Val."

She touched her father's arm. "Would you like me to pray with you, Daddy?"

Tears of remorse filled his eyes. "Yes, my Valentine. Pray for your sinful father and share one of those hugs he needs so badly."

She held on tightly, wishing she could absorb his pain, and whispered, "He can't help it, Daddy. He's a sick old man. Let's pray that God works in his life in a miraculous way."

"That's a prayer I've prayed many times."

She grasped her father's hands in hers. "Blessed heavenly Father, we come to You today seeking healing for Mathias Truelove. Free him from his bondage of sin and help him understand You are all he needs in this life to be content. We ask the miracle of a changed life for our loved one. Direct his path to You. And, Lord, give my father peace in this situation. As always, thank You for the blessings You bestow on us daily and the gift You gave us with Your Son, Jesus Christ. Amen."

Her father joined in with a heartfelt amen. "Thank you, Val. I'm sorry I reacted so badly."

"Never be sorry, Daddy. You're the best

father any children ever had. When I see you hurting because of Granddaddy, it breaks my heart that you didn't have what we have."

He hugged her again. "Thanks, Valentine. I'd better get to work."

"I love you, Daddy."

He touched her cheek. "I love you, too."

After he left, Val found her thoughts on her dad's pain. She knew it must run deep for him to behave so out of character. He'd never forbidden her to do anything. He had asked her not to do things, and out of respect she'd done as he requested, just as she would in this situation.

She wondered what she could do to help heal the rift between them. Val feared it would never happen as long as her father and grandfather refused to communicate.

Picking up the phone, she dialed Maddy's office. After talking to her replacement for a couple of minutes, she asked to speak to her former boss. They exchanged pleasantries, and Val said, "I wondered if you had time to discuss a plan I feel could be mutually beneficial."

"Sure. Can you come by Thursday morning? Ten thirty would be good for me. I have a lunch appointment with the Jensens, and I know it will probably run well over into the afternoon."

"See you then."

As she drove the familiar route to Lexington later that week, Val considered Maddy's reaction to her proposal. Would her former boss be willing to refer her wedding parties to Your Wedding Place?

Over the years she'd heard Maddy complain about the lack of wedding venues available to brides who didn't want a traditional church wedding or reception. Val had always been on the lookout for unique places. If she read about something in a local magazine, she'd kept a record for when there was a need. A number of brides had been very receptive to the places she found.

Val parked behind the beautifully renovated old house off Main Street and went inside.

Maddy greeted her with a hug and invited her to sit in the visitor chair. She chose the other chair, setting a casual tone for the meeting. "So what have you been up to now that you're a lady of leisure?"

Val's life had become even more hectic since leaving her job back in the spring. "Busier than ever. I wanted to talk to you because I think we can help each other." She pulled a brochure from her bag. "I'm in the process of putting together a business called Your Wedding Place."

Noting the look of concern on Maddy's face, Val quickly explained, "Not from the wedding planner aspect. I wouldn't do that to you. I promise to refer brides regardless of whether my idea interests you or not."

Maddy smiled her relief. "Thank you for that."

"You know I think you're an excellent wedding planner," Val told her.

"I enjoy the challenge."

Val handed her the pamphlet she'd picked up from the printer just that morning. "That's why I wanted to share my idea." She launched into the presentation she'd prepared. "I know how difficult it is to find adequate venues. What we hope to do at Your Wedding Place is create a variety that appeals to many couples."

As Maddy studied the pamphlet, Val pulled a business card from her pocket. She'd hired a publicist who had created the brochure, business cards, and even her Web site, which would go live once she finalized the plans.

Maddy tapped the brochure. "This is impressive, Val."

"Thank you. There are a number of expansion plans in the works. We hope to complete this structure later this year. It will be the perfect outdoor wedding or reception site for spring, summer, and milder fall weather."

"Incredible," Maddy commented.

"It's all thanks to you."

Maddy's familiar droll smile flashed as she said, "Guess that's one gift that will keep on giving."

Val nodded. In more ways than Maddy could begin to know. "That's why I'd like to continue working with you. I think we could benefit each other."

"Would I be your only wedding planner?"

"Exclusivity might not work well in this situation," Val told her. "I want to schedule enough weddings to keep the profit margin in the black, and I think that would require doing business with more than one planner."

"The premise is huge. What happens when the wedding party exceeds what you have to offer?"

"We have the house and gardens, and I'm considering adding another structure large enough to hold cold-weather or large indoor receptions. I'd also like to build a small chapel."

"Are you limiting yourself to locals who want unique sites?"

Val shook her head. "Not totally. There

are hotels in Paris and Lexington that would enable us to bring in larger parties willing to accept inconvenience for originality."

"I think it's a great idea, Val. And I'll be glad to add you to my vendor list."

"I'd pay you a percentage for referrals. We'll discuss that once things are further along."

"Are you ready to book now? I have a small wedding that's looking for a place. The bride wants a garden wedding, but we haven't found exactly what she wants."

"What date? I have an August wedding booked for the English garden."

Maddy stood and moved around her desk to check her planner. She named the date.

"That's the week after the other wedding. You want to bring the couple out to see the gardens? We're working in the English and Japanese gardens."

"I'd love to see the place," Maddy said. "You deserve this, Val. I've recognized your potential for years. You're an admirable young woman." When she blushed, Maddy insisted, "It's true. I've never known anyone to make the sacrifices you made for your siblings. How is everyone?"

Another sibling might harbor bad feelings, but not Val. As the oldest of seven kids she'd decided not to burden her parents with her college expenses. Instead, she'd worked and taken night courses to obtain her associate degree in business. After graduation she'd gone to work as Maddy's assistant.

Jacob and Cindy Truelove worked hard at raising a very close-knit family. They had taught their children the importance of helping each other in whatever life brought their way. The idea of burdening Opie and the twins with student loans had prompted Val to continue to live at home, drive a secondhand car, and use the majority of her salary to support their educational endeavors. She had no doubt they in turn would help their younger siblings and their parents.

"They all have their own plans for where they might fit into the business. Rom and Heath have been helping with my business plan. Opie's considering her options."

"Your mom should open a floral design shop. She'd do an incredible job," Maddy said. They had called upon Cindy Truelove's considerable talent a few times when they had a bride in a pinch.

"She would." The grandfather clock gonged, and Val glanced up. "I've taken enough of your time." Val slid her purse up her arm as she stood. "I'd appreciate it if you kept this confidential. We're still in the planning and legal stages."

"Certainly. I'll be in touch about the garden. Is there a time that's better for you?"

"Tomorrow or Saturday would be fine. Just let me know."

"I'll call you with a time after I speak with the bride."

The meeting had gone exactly as she'd hoped. "Thanks again, Maddy."

Val was still smiling when she closed the door and stepped into the hallway she had traversed many times.

"Well, if isn't Ms. Moneybags. What brings you down to your old stomping grounds?"

Derrick's sneer reminded Val of the numerous run-ins she'd had with the office Casanova. No doubt he'd gotten the message and reverted to his previous nasty self.

"I had an appointment with Maddy."

"Giving back some of that money?"

"It's really none of your business, Derrick."

"I worked just as hard as you did on that wedding. I deserve that money as much as you do."

Val had helped a couple of her former coworkers who had real needs, but that wasn't his concern. "I suppose that's why they call gambling chance. I prayed and believed God would provide. As answers to prayers go, it was a big one."

"Prayers," he repeated, spitting the word like one of the four-letter words he used regularly. "Winning the lottery doesn't have anything to do with prayer. It's luck."

"Call it what you will, Derrick, but I consider the money an answer to a prayer. A blessing, in fact."

"So why don't you share your blessing? I could use a million or two."

The way he said blessing bothered Val. She knew from experience that Derrick's lifestyle left no time for the Lord. "What do you need, Derrick?" If he could list one worthwhile thing, she'd happily hand over the funds.

"A new car would be a start."

She recalled how he had walked into the office bragging about his new sports car just this past January. Derrick's expensive lifestyle took every dime he made and more. Val didn't doubt he was deep in debt. "What's wrong with the car you have?"

"It's got expensive payments, honey. Ties up funds I could be spending on the ladies."

His evil leer made chill bumps appear on Val's arms. She rubbed them away, wishing he'd leave. Instead he leaned against the doorway, blocking her exit. "It was your choice, Derrick. Did it ever occur to you that I drove my old car and worked to have money to help my family?"

"Oh come on, Val. That holier-than-thou attitude of yours is wearing thin. Tell me you're not enjoying that lottery win."

"Not in situations like this," she emphasized. "Life is not a free ride, Derrick. Every decision has consequences."

"Yeah, like it took some big decision to accept that money," he mocked.

"Believe it or not, it did. I knew it would change our lives forever. And not all for the good. That's why I have no intention of wasting the money on senseless purchases."

He straightened up and leaned forward. "Doing something nice for me wouldn't be senseless."

"You're right." Val dragged her purse around and pulled out ten dollars. "Here, Derrick. Have lunch on me."

"You little — !" he shouted.

Maddy's office door swung open. "What's going on here?"

"Ah, Val and I were talking."

A flash of sympathy crossed Maddy's face. "I'm sorry, Val. Please step into my office, Derrick."

His expression spoke volumes as he maneuvered past Val, pausing long enough to snatch the money from her hand.

"See you soon, Val," Maddy said with a smile before closing the door.

When the woman leaving Maddy Troyer's office charged into him on the sidewalk, Russ didn't know what to think. He grabbed her arms to keep them both standing and did a double take.

"Val?" Russ said, taken aback by her appearance. A suit and heels had replaced the scruffy jeans.

"Excuse me," she said, somewhat breathlessly. She looked up. "Oh, Russ. Hi."

He let go and stepped back. "I planned to call you later to discuss the plans. Care to join me for a working lunch?" As he watched her face transform with her smile, Russ lost his focus. "I'm sorry. What did you say?"

"I asked where you wanted to eat."

"Actually I thought we might have lunch in our conference room. I can ask our secretary to order something for us."

"Why don't we just pick up a Jack's Burger? My treat," she offered.

"Sounds good," Russ agreed.

Inside the small but popular burger joint, they studied the menu board and chose the chiliburger special.

"No doubt it will end up on the front of my clothes, but I do love this burger."

"Extra napkins," Russ told the woman at the counter.

"Lots of them," Val added with a big smile.

They stepped over to the pickup area to wait for their order.

"Nice weather we're having," Russ said as they sat on a bench and watched the other patrons come and go.

"Beautiful. I've made good progress in the gardens the past couple of days."

"What happened to the Sheridans' gardener?"

"There hasn't been one for years," Val told him. "Mr. Sheridan never cared for the gardens as much as his wife. The people he hired did an absolute minimum."

"You should hire a landscaper."

"We can have it finished by the time I explain to someone else what needs to be done," Val said. "Mrs. Sheridan taught us a lot about gardening. She really loved Heath. During the summers she'd send for him, and he got out of the chores."

"Considering the size of those gardens, I'd think the chores would have been easier."

"Heath loved helping her. He'd make suggestions, and it thrilled him when she liked his ideas."

"Must feel good to own the place now,"

Russ said.

"It does."

The clerk called number thirty-nine. "That's us," Russ said, jumping up to claim the bags. He carried them down the street and held the door for her to enter Prestige Designs. The office occupied the building next door to Madeline Troyer's Event Planning. Val had walked past it many times, never thinking that one day they would be working for her.

"Thanks for agreeing to this," Russ said. "Cheryl, Ms. Truelove and I will be meeting in the conference room."

Taken aback by the woman's unfriendly glare, Val smiled and responded to Russ. "No problem. I was in Lexington anyway."

"When you came storming out of Maddy's, I didn't realize it was you."

"I had a run-in with a former coworker."

Russ indicated the small conference room. "We'll meet in here. The restroom is just down the hall. I'll grab my plans and be right back."

He returned a few minutes later with a man he introduced as Randall King.

"Welcome to Prestige Designs, Ms. Truelove. It's a pleasure to meet you in person."

"You, too, Mr. King."

"I trust Russ is treating you well. He's

filled me in on your plans for Sheridan Farm. I must say they are most ambitious."

"But achievable?"

The enigmatic expression on his face said little. "With good planning and sufficient funds most things are achievable."

"That's what I thought."

He nodded at the food emitting delicious scents into the room. "I see you've planned a working lunch."

"We did," Russ said.

"Then don't let me keep you. In fact, I'm inspired to dash over for a burger of my own. I look forward to our future meetings, Ms. Truelove."

Val nodded. After his boss left, Russ opened his burger wrapper and took a big bite of the sandwich. Uncharacteristic silence filled the room. "Is something wrong?"

"It's been one of those days. Something happened before I left home this morning that's weighing heavy on my mind and heart. I've given it over to God, but you know how it is."

Russ shrugged and shook his head. "Can't say that I do. There's no aspect of my life I expect God to shoulder."

"I can't imagine life without my Savior. No matter how bad things get, He's there for me."

"And yet you're troubled?"

"Not because I doubt God will handle things," Val assured him. "I hurt for Daddy."

"Your father? Why?"

"He doesn't have a good relationship with his father, and it hurts him. I hate seeing him so unhappy."

Russ shrugged. "Lots of us don't get along with family, but we get by."

"He's a Christian, Russ. The Bible speaks very strongly about being at odds with your brother."

Russ balled up the sandwich wrapper and laid it on the table. "Guess I'll never be a Christian then. I don't have any qualms about not associating with Wendell."

"It doesn't bother you at all?" Val asked. "Don't you miss having him in your life?"

"Not particularly. We were never friends."

"I can't imagine not having a relationship with my family."

"You'd think differently if one of them stabbed you in the back."

" 'And unto him that smiteth thee on one cheek offer also the other; and him that taketh away thy cloak forbid not to take thy coat also,' " Val said, quoting Luke 6:29.

He wiped his mouth. "Nice sentiment but impossible to live by. No one turns the other cheek. Nor do they give up what's rightfully theirs. Does your father see your grand-father?"

"Not often. Grandfather has spent the last thirty years in prison. Daddy's concerned because he thinks Grandfather knows I won the lottery. He's afraid he'll try to get money from me."

"Sounds like a user. Your dad's entitled to feel as he does. I know what that's like. Wendell took advantage of the situation and didn't bother to think about me. Why should I care about him?"

"Because he's your brother," Val insisted.

Russ reached for the plans and spread them across the tabletop, effectively con-cluding the conversation. Her gaze followed as he indicated the property layout and the code requirements for the parking area and green space.

"I want one large parking area over here." She pointed out the location on the map. "Once on the property all guests will be transported to their wedding sites."

"I wish you'd mentioned that earlier," he said, a touch of irritation in his tone.

"Perhaps you should have inquired."

Her comment reminded Russ of his re-sponsibility to guide her through the pro-cess.

"Eat your burger before it gets cold." Val turned the pages until she reached the one showing the structure. Russ noticed she ate little as she studied the prints.

"I like the way you've placed this so the structure is here, overlooking the view."

"That's what you wanted, right?" Russ didn't care for the uncertainty that plagued him with this project. He'd never felt like this before. Determined not to disappoint her again, he'd worked and reworked his designs.

"Yes. What are we calling this?"

"I'm fairly certain the project will be classified as Assembly Group. What we call it depends on how we finish the upper floor. We could use columns and make it a colonnade, or we can use arches and canopies and call it a pavilion. Custom ironwork could be used for a top to keep it more open."

"Which do you suggest?"

"A colonnade would have a more formal feel while the ironwork would make this much more open and informal. I have a couple of plans to show you today."

She looked shocked. Russ suspected she'd been certain he'd never get what she wanted.

"I'm ready whenever you are."

Russ had exerted a great deal of extra effort on the plans. He'd even taken time to color in the scenic view in the distance on the landscaping plan.

"What are these?" she asked, pointing to the low line below the platform. "Windows?"

"Yes," Russ said, pleased she'd noticed. "I understand placement is primary, but I tried to anticipate a few other things. You can't have groups of people out there without facilities, so I thought of ways we could work those in and best benefit your business. I put all the mechanicals and bathrooms underneath, along with a large indoor area you can use for inclement weather receptions. I made the structure accessible with the ramp and an elevator here," he said, indicating them on the plan. "And I worked in a good-sized kitchen with fridges and ice machines. The facilities would enable caterers to store their food on site. You can rent the space to those who want accessibility."

"I hadn't thought of that," Val said.

"And then there's the storage issue. I know you plan to store tables, chairs, and linens elsewhere on the property, but think of the time involved in moving the items.

Having them on-site would be your best option."

"You've really thought this through," Val said.

"I think raising the structure like this and giving it a rooftop overlook not only enhances the scenery but makes the view even more incredible."

"But won't the raised height require railings?" Val asked. "Those don't fit the open concept I wanted."

"The basic premise of a colonnade is rows of columns at several intervals that support a roof," Russ explained. "I had considered balustrades in areas, but we could look into less visual options if you like the idea. What do you think about graduated steps on the end going out toward a small ornamental water feature?"

"What if we continued the steps with a patio around the structure?" Val asked. "It wouldn't need to be large. Lounge areas are popular with wedding guests. Where would the band be?"

"Here," Russ said, tapping the area along the back of the colonnade. "The dance floor is there. If you want, you could use interchangeable tiles to change designs based on your clients' requests. Wiring and lighting could be run in the posts and beams along the top of the structure."

"I like it," Val said.

Russ nearly sighed with relief.

She glanced at him. "What was your other idea?"

He pulled over another plan, not opening it. "Colonnade, one level, facilities in free-standing structure, no underground construction." He tapped the first plan. "This allows you to offer more options to the brides."

"What's the construction time frame?"

"A basement and elevator will lengthen the project time but definitely class up the structure."

"You're sure we can do a basement?"

"We'd need to do a feasibility study."

"I want to hire smaller local companies to do the work."

"I think that would be a mistake," Russ offered. "Larger contractors are better equipped to deal with some of the issues that might arise. If it's a matter of saving money —"

"No," Val interrupted. "It's a matter of helping smaller companies attain higher profit levels because they're given the opportunity. Some of these companies are as good or better than their larger counterparts."

"I still think a larger company, like Kevin Flint's, could do the job more effectively," Russ declared.

"But that's not what your client wants," Val said firmly.

"Okay, I'll hire someone to do the study. Then we'll find your contractor." He started rolling the plans for Val to take with her. "We could request the contractor subcontract smaller companies."

Val pushed their wrappings from lunch into the bag. "And watch them walk away with the profit. I want the smaller companies to benefit from the project. Truelove Inc. will adhere to this policy consistently, so if you can't work with that I'll pay for the plans and find someone else to carry them through."

"I'm just offering alternatives."

"And I appreciate that, but there are some things I will not vary from." Her eyes drifted back to the plans. "You did an excellent job with these, Russ. What helped you see the vision?"

"Your window-to-the-world comment."

"I'm definitely pleased. You've solved two problems with the basement structure. I can't wait to show the family."

"I hope they like what they see."

"Why don't you come for dinner and hear

their thoughts for yourself? You could answer any questions they might have."

Kelly had been right. Val planned to involve her entire family. "When?"

"Tonight. Just a family dinner. Nothing fancy."

Russ shrugged. "I'd love to hear what they have to say."

SEVEN

"Val, talk to your father. He won't listen to me," Cindy Truelove said, her green gaze never leaving her husband's face.

Val always found it humorous that her mother thought she could make her father do something when he wouldn't listen to his wife. She had arrived home only minutes before and gone in to tell her mother about their dinner guest.

"I won't have it," Jacob Truelove insisted. "No one comes on this farm acting like that man did."

"What man?" Val asked. "What happened?"

"Some stranger showed up earlier today, using foul language and making threats against you."

"You have no idea who he was?" Val asked.

"No. Nearly ran Clyde down with his flashy red sports car. When I shouted at him, he cursed at me."

"Can you describe him?" Val asked, almost certain she knew who the man was.

"Short guy. Blond hair. Wore a suit. Wanted to know where you were. Said it was your fault and you owed him. What did he mean?"

"Sounds like Derrick from Maddy's office." Val recounted the earlier incident. "I didn't do anything to him."

"He obviously thinks you did. I told him he's not welcome here."

"Heath told him the same thing recently."

"He's been here before?" her father demanded.

Val nodded. "He asked me out several times and wouldn't accept no for an answer. He got nervous when Heath suggested he move on. Said we were all crazy before he jumped in his car and drove off. He was his usual nasty self at the office today."

"Since when does no one tell me these things?" her father inquired irritably.

Val smiled. "Heath offered to introduce him to you and Rom. That's when Derrick opted to leave."

"Here, Jacob," her mother said when she returned with a glass of ice water. "Drink this and cool off."

"I'll check in with Maddy and see if she knows anything about what's going on."

Val pulled her cell phone from her purse, realizing she'd never turned it back on after her meeting. She saw she had a message and after listening knew why Derrick was so angry. "Maddy fired him. She says her decision had nothing to do with me."

"Then why does he blame you?" her dad asked.

"Derrick would never blame himself. I'm sure I became the perfect scapegoat since he was arguing with me when Maddy called him into the office."

"I will not tolerate him coming onto this property and communicating threats. I'm contacting the sheriff."

While she knew it was the smart thing to do, Val dreaded involving the police. No doubt it would only fuel Derrick's anger. Resigned, she said, "I invited Russ Hunter to dinner tonight. I'll call and cancel. He can show you all the plans another time."

"No, don't," her father and mother said at the same time. Val looked from one to the other.

"Opie and I cooked a big dinner."

"And I want to see these plans," her dad added. "I know you're anxious to get started."

"Are you sure?" Val felt uncertain.

"Positive," he said.

"I'd better check the ham. Opie's been after me all afternoon to let her try something different."

After her mother left the room again, Val said, "I should have known Derrick would do something after the way he attacked me today."

"Attacked?"

"Verbal assault," she explained quickly. "He cornered me in the hallway and asked for money. Seemed to think I should subsidize his womanizing with my winnings."

"Womanizing?" Her father's expression changed to that of defender. "What did he say to you, Valentine?"

"Derrick got nasty when I explained the money was a blessing. Said that ticket could have just as easily been his and I should do something nice for him. I gave him ten dollars and suggested he treat himself to lunch."

"That doesn't sound like you, Val."

"He brings out the worst in me. And I don't think Maddy appreciated his poorloser behavior either."

"I knew this would happen."

"I've tried to be nice to Derrick, Daddy. Some of my friends from work say he's implied things about me that weren't true."

"Why didn't you tell me this before?"

She heaved a sigh. "Because I'm a grown woman who can't come running to you every time some guy insults me."

"You can always come to me, Val. And your brothers. Any of us would have had a talk with him."

"You can't reason with Derrick. We should look into security. Make sure no one comes onto the farm without clearance at the front gate. Next time he could cause real harm."

"There won't be a next time. I plan to make sure he knows he's not welcome here."

"You don't think we need security?"

"Yes, I do. I suspect the farm is only going to become even more active, and security will make us and your brides feel protected. Even more so once those expensive building supplies start coming in. And we should hire a bodyguard for you."

He had really kicked into protective father mode. "I don't need a bodyguard," Val protested.

"You didn't before the money."

"I'll be more cautious, Daddy. Make sure everyone knows where I am when I leave the farm."

"People know you are wealthy, Val. Even if we discount this man, others are willing to do harm for money. I think we should hire a driver to accompany you when you're out on your own."

"In my old car? That would look ridiculous."

"You can afford to upgrade."

His comment surprised Val. One thing they had agreed upon was that they wouldn't flaunt their wealth. No world travels, no expensive wardrobes or costly toys, just basic needs and helping others. The only truly frivolous thing she'd done was buy that date for Opie, and even that had supported a worthwhile charity.

"And call even more attention to myself?"

"I doubt you could get more attention. Think it over. I'll check into security for the farm."

"I can do it if you like," Val said, feeling guilty to have added yet another burden to her father's load. "You already have plenty on your plate. Speaking of plates, I should help with dinner since I invited a guest."

"Seems that fellow is coming here pretty often," her father commented.

"I ran into him this morning, and he showed me the redesigned plans. They're good, Daddy. I want everyone's input before they're finalized."

"You think he can handle the Truelove gang?"

Val laughed. "He had lunch with four of

us the other day and survived."

"That says something for him," he said. "Get the phone book. I'll call a few security firms while you help your mom and Opie prepare dinner for your young man."

"He's not my young man," Val objected.

"Well, he's certainly not mine," her father said, laughter booming when Val punched him playfully on the arm.

"By the way, you got a special delivery letter today. I put it on the entry hall table."

"Thanks, Daddy. I'll check it out later."

More dread than peace filled Russ as he drove to Paris that night. After Val left, Randall King had summoned him to his office. "How did it go?"

"She's pleased with the plans. She asked me to make a presentation to her family tonight after dinner."

"Good. Recommend Kevin Flint as the contractor."

"I already did. She refused."

Randall frowned. "What do you mean she refused?"

"Val plans to give her business to smaller contractors. Feels it's important that others who are less fortunate benefit from her investment."

"We always use Kevin. I expect you to

convince her his is the best firm for the job."

"I've tried."

Randall King didn't look pleased. "Get the final plan approval. I'll deal with this."

Russ didn't understand why Mr. King suddenly insisted on becoming involved in this project. Val wasn't going to appreciate his interference. Not one bit. As he drove down the driveway, the setting sun formed the perfect backdrop behind the Sheridan mansion. He took the road that led to the manager's house and parked. Pulling the plans from the backseat, Russ walked to the door and knocked.

"Hi. Come on in." Val held the screen door open.

"Are you sure about this?"

"Just think of it as a dinner meeting," she suggested. "Different clientele but you don't have to pick up the tab."

"That's a first," he agreed, smiling at her joke.

"Dinner's ready," her mother called.

As they walked into the dining room, he noted the scramble for chairs. Val tapped the young man Russ assumed to be a younger brother on the shoulder and indicated he should find another chair. "Sit here, next to Daddy."

Russ looked at the boy and shrugged. His

smile resembled Val's as he quickly found another seat.

"Cy likes to sit in Rom's place," she explained. "He'll have to adjust now that they're home again."

Russ noted their absence. "Where are Rom and Heath?"

"Tying up loose ends in Boston. They'll be home by the weekend."

The noise died down, and when her father reached for his hand, Russ pulled back. Jacob Truelove wasn't deterred and firmly grasped his hand.

"Grace," Val whispered, taking Russ's other hand and reaching for Opie's hand. After blessing the food, they began passing bowls. As the food moved around the table, Val quickly introduced everyone.

"Roc, leave some of those potatoes for our guest."

"Ah, Mom, you know I love your potatoes," he said, giving up the bowl.

She winked at him and scooped her serving onto his plate before serving her husband and handing the bowl over to Russ.

"Val tells me you showed her the plans today," Jacob said as he carved the ham.

He nodded. "The revised plans. She thought you might like to look them over."

"Can I see, too?" Jules asked. Val nodded.

Her sister talked about becoming an architect and was very interested in her plans for the farm.

"Speaking of plans, what do you think about my converting one of the outbuildings into a restaurant?" Opie asked. "I'd need to get financing, but I think it could work."

Russ noted the way Val glanced at her parents and back at Opie before she asked, "Are you sure? I thought you wanted to expand your horizons."

"I want to cook," Opie said. "And I've pretty much decided I can be happier here with my family than off somewhere missing all of you."

"We could find a restaurant in Lexington or Paris," Val said, taking the potatoes Russ offered. "Financing won't be as difficult as you fear. I've set aside monetary gifts for all three graduates."

"No, Val," she said without hesitation. "You've done enough."

She grimaced playfully at Opie. "I have to give you something, and you can use the money to get what you want."

"It's a loan, Val. I intend to repay every dime," Opie declared.

"Not your graduation gift."

"You're so stubborn."

"Wonder where I get it from," Val countered with a grin.

"All of you get it from your father," her mother teased, smiling at her husband.

"Hey, now," their father said in mock affront. "In my family it's called determination."

After the laughter died down, Opie said, "I could offer catering services to Your Wedding Place clientele."

"Won't that be too much?"

"Not if I hire sufficient staff. They should be able to work out of my restaurant kitchens."

Val smiled at her sister, and Russ paused in forking food into his mouth. He'd never witnessed such love between family members.

Their mother cleared her throat. "Heath talked to me last week, and he wants to handle the landscaping for your business."

"Landscaping? With an MBA?" Val questioned.

Her mother nodded. "You know how much he enjoys working outside. I think he let Rom convince him a degree in business would benefit the family more."

"Following his heart would have cost much less."

"Heath appreciates the sacrifices you

made, Val. He fully intends to use his degree, but he wants to help you get your business off the ground. You know he took those landscape design courses at UK."

Val nodded. "He has excellent ideas. Heath always grew the biggest flowers and the best vegetables."

"Remember that year he decided to give Mom a rose garden for Mother's Day?" Opie asked.

"We begged him to let us help."

"Not that hard," Opie said. "He loved telling us what to do."

"That garden still brings tears to my eyes," Cindy Truelove said.

"It brought a few tears to my eyes, too," Opie said.

"Only because you wanted to make mud pies instead of planting flowers," Val teased.

Opie laughed. "I knew what I wanted even then. So can we work together?"

"We'll talk," Val promised. "Though I think you'll be too busy once you get involved with the restaurant."

"The kitchen area in the structure's lower floor could be used for catering," Russ said.

Opie looked interested. "There's a kitchen?"

Russ swallowed hastily. "Big sinks, prep area, industrial fridges, pantry storage, and countertops. We could add a commercial stove or two."

"It wouldn't be a restaurant," Val pointed out.

"I like the idea though," Opie told her. "Where exactly will these facilities be?"

"Right here at Sheridan Farm. In the basement of the new structure," Russ told her. "That gives Val an inclement weather area now rather than later."

"Wow. Sounds like these plans have come a long way," Opie exclaimed. When Val looked at her, she grimaced. "I mean . . . well, you said you were reworking the plan."

Russ chuckled. "I hope I've improved from those first attempts to capture Val's vision."

After they cleared the table, everyone settled in their seats for a Truelove family discussion. Russ spread the plans across the table, and the brainstorming was nonstop. Cindy poured coffee and looked over her husband's shoulder as he pointed out things he thought would improve the flow.

As planning sessions went, Russ found their input very productive. He'd notated nearly two full pages on his legal pad before realizing how late it was. When he said he needed to call it a night, Val walked him to his car.

"I'll call you tomorrow to discuss those changes."

He nodded. "Thanks for dinner. I enjoyed meeting your parents and the younger members of your family. I've never met a group that loves each other like you do."

"I don't know what I'd do without them."

"You're fortunate," Russ said. "They all want to help you succeed. Wish I could say the same."

"Would you like to talk about it?"

"It's past history. Wendell goes his way, and I go mine, and we're content with that."

"Are you really? I can't imagine any circumstance that would make me feel good about being estranged from my siblings."

"Give it time. Eventually one of them will do or say something to make you rethink that. Particularly now that money is involved. I never would have thought Wendell would stab me in the back, but he did."

"It's only land, Russ. He's your brother."

"Then why did he grab everything for himself? He knew I loved the farm."

Val shrugged. "Have you asked him?"

"There's nothing left to say."

"Being stubborn will hurt you more. Don't make that a reason not to see each other."

"I won't pretend everything is okay. Once

I'm established I'll buy a place of my own. And when I have kids I won't play favorites."

"I should tell you Opie had a date with your brother Tuesday night."

"She went out with Wendell?"

Val nodded. "I bought her a date with him."

He started to say something and stopped, puzzled by Val's words. "Bought a date?"

"At a bachelor auction. Paris's most eligible bachelors. It was for a good cause."

"Why would you do that?" Russ demanded.

"You wouldn't understand."

"You think you can heal the rift between us. Well, you can't," Russ said, stomping off toward his car.

Val chased after him. "You didn't have anything to do with this."

She almost ran into him when he stopped. "What do you mean?"

"It was payback," Val admitted with embarrassment. "Remember when Opie invited you to join us for lunch?" He nodded, and Val said, "Frankly I wasn't a fan at the time. When she asked you to join us I promised retribution."

"You said it was okay."

"What else could I say?" There was a subtle challenge in her tone. "We've pulled practical jokes on each other for years. Opie showed me this man in the magazine and said his views on women were archaic. When the Hunter name started popping up around me, I admit to being curious. I suggested we attend, and after I bought the date she said she wouldn't go."

"But she did?"

Val nodded. "I think she feels challenged to divest him of his outdated views."

"Good luck. He's his father's son."

"So are you."

"I'm nothing like Wendell. I don't understand you," Russ declared curtly.

"Same here," Val returned.

Curious, he asked, "Are you still not a fan of mine?"

She shrugged and looked down at the ground. "You were such a pompous windbag that first meeting, challenging my plans and acting like owning a Kentucky farm gave you some sort of God-given right to tell me what to do."

Russ sighed heavily. "That attitude could have cost me my job. I've been warned about expressing my opinion to clients."

"You still get above your raising now and then, but I think I'm beginning to understand you better," she said matter-of-factly.

"Wendell at a bachelor auction," he said

with a shake of his head. "Never thought I'd hear that."

"Perhaps you should sign up for the next fund-raiser."

"I don't live in Paris."

"You were raised here. I'm sure they'd consider you."

"No, thanks. I have no interest in being shown like a prize stallion."

"Whoa! Who has a major opinion of himself?" Val teased.

"You know what I mean," Russ said, thankful the darkness hid his embarrassment.

"I'd bid on you," she offered with a little laugh.

"You don't have to buy a date. I'll take you out anytime you like."

"I didn't mean . . . ," Val stuttered.

"I did," Russ said. "Name the date, and I'll prove I know how to show a woman a good time."

"I'm holding you up when . . . you need to get home," Val stammered. "We have the contractor coming early tomorrow to look at the renovations."

Russ nodded his head toward the Sheridan mansion. "I still say that's where you need to be. You really want to, don't you? Tell the truth."

"It's a beautiful home."

"That needs to be occupied. Spending thousands in renovations when that house is already here doesn't strike me as a wise investment."

"Mom would probably go if Daddy would agree."

"You should ask again. You never know. He might have changed his mind."

"I suppose I could. Thanks again, Russ."

"No problem. I'll be in touch tomorrow about those changes, and then we'll see what we can do to get the project under-way."

"I'll look forward to your call."

And she would, Val realized as she watched his car taillights disappear into the night. She thought about Russ's feelings toward his brother. What could she do to help the situation? Only one answer came to mind, and she promised to pray for them both.

Back inside she saw the letter her dad had mentioned earlier on the entry table. The return address read KFD Corporation. She opened the envelope and scanned the contents, finding an offer to purchase Sheridan Farm at a price slightly lower than they had paid.

She found her father in his recliner, reading the newspaper. "Take a look at this," she said, passing him the letter.

He read it quickly and handed it back. "I suppose we'll see a few of those over the years."

"How did they know to address it to me? I doubt the tax records show us as the owners."

"I'm sure they did their research," her father said. "Does it bother you?"

She shrugged. "Not really. So what did you think of Russ's plans?"

"The basement is a good idea. If you drop the height on that platform you could avoid having barricades around the structure."

"What about Opie's idea? You think she can make it work?"

"I don't doubt any of my children can do anything they put their minds to. Opie's been a little flighty over the years, but cooking is the one thing she's stuck with. And she's good."

"I can see the benefit of having her here. In fact, I'd be willing to finance her restaurant."

"I don't think she wants you to do that," her dad said.

"I intend to give them money for graduation gifts."

He nodded. "Will you let Heath help you?"

"Even if I do think he's offering out of guilt, I'd be an idiot to say no. He knows those gardens so well."

"I'm sure he has his reasons. All of us want you to do well, Valentine. And if Heath gets to enjoy himself while helping you, I'd say he's the winner."

Her father had a point. For the first time in their lives they had the luxury of time to decide their futures. "I'm glad Russ got those plans worked out. I thought I would have to contact his boss."

Her dad winked at her. "Oh, I don't know. A pretty Truelove woman can generally get what she wants out of a man without threats."

"All I want from Russ is a finished set of plans," she persisted.

"I like him," her father said. "He got along well with the family and didn't seem to mind answering all those questions Jules shot his way. He made a friend for life when he invited her to his office."

"But he really harbors bad feelings toward his brother, and he's so secretive. I'm used to saying what we have to say and moving on."

"It's a rare family that can do that, Val."

Communication was a gift. "He made a good point tonight about renovations being a waste when we already have the big house. He thinks it deserves to be loved by a family again."

"Is that what you think?"

She hesitated. "I think maybe we should give it further consideration. We'll sink thousands into renovating this place when we already own the perfect house."

"We don't need the renovations, Val. This home has served us well for years."

"But the Sheridans' house has pluses, too. More room for the family. The security system. This house will be smaller with four adult children living here."

"Perhaps the adult children should consider living in the big house?" her father suggested with a raised brow.

"Not without everyone else," she protested.

He grinned. "I told you before, Val. If it's what the family wants, I'll go."

"Will you talk to Mom?"

"If you tell me why you want to move."

She must be as transparent as glass. "I love that house," Val said simply. "I have ever since I can remember. Living there would be a dream come true."

"Have you sought God's will in the matter?"

"Probably not as much as I should."

"Let's pray over it and hear what the contractor has to say tomorrow. If the Lord convicts us that it's His will, I'll talk to your mom."

Val hugged him. "Thanks, Daddy. I think I'll go talk to Opie about her plans."

She walked down the hallway to the room she shared with her sisters. Wrapped in her robe with a towel around her head, Opie sat on the bed polishing her toenails. She glanced up. "Russ get off okay?"

"Why wouldn't he?" Val asked.

"I thought maybe his head had exploded from all those questions Jules asked," Opie remarked, dodging the stuffed animal Jules threw at her. "He had a distinct deer-in-the-headlights look a few times there when all of us got started."

Jules grabbed her robe and headed for the shower, leaving them alone.

"I think it came closer to bursting when I told him you went out with Wendell." Val dropped down on her bed. "He accused me of trying to interfere in their relationship."

"What did you say to that?"

"That it had nothing to do with him."

Opie removed the towel and fluffed the damp tendrils. "Russ gets along well with the family, don't you think?"

Val refused to let her matchmaking family

131

push her in that direction. Russ Hunter might be on her mind a lot lately, but their relationship was business.

Wasn't it? "If you're so determined to play matchmaker, why don't you work on Heath and Jane?"

"Is that why you made her your assistant?"

"She needed the job, and I know she'll be an asset. She has a lot of managerial experience. Just wait. You'll see how good she is."

"Have you seen how Heath looks at her?" Opie asked.

"I think he's always had a crush on Jane but thought she was out of his league."

"And now she's going to be working here all day while he's landscaping your project."

"I don't know about that, Opie," Val said, expressing her concern. "I can't reconcile his spending years in college to come home and landscape."

"You heard what Mom said. It's Heath's choice."

"But is he doing it for the right reason?"

"You told Rom he had time when he went for the interview. Why not offer Heath the same option?"

Opie had a point. "I'll talk to him. Is this restaurant what you want to do?"

She shrugged. "Ideas are bouncing around in my head faster than I can process. Even more since Russ mentioned expanding the kitchen in the structure. I could run a catering business from there."

"You just like the idea of having a commercial kitchen at your disposal," Val teased.

"Every chef's dream," Opie agreed.

"Nothing has to be decided right away."

Opie pumped lotion into her hand and smoothed it over her arms and legs. "Russ really redeemed himself with that plan today, didn't he?"

"Yes," Val said. "I couldn't believe you said what you did."

Opie grinned. "Sorry. It slipped out. I tried to backpedal."

Val giggled. "We noticed. When I looked at the plans I knew my brides would experience my feelings when they stood on that overlook." She hesitated. "Opie, what do you think about moving into the Sheridans' house?"

Her head popped up. "Having my own bedroom? Sign me up."

"Daddy and I are praying over the situation. Will you pray, too?"

Opie nodded.

"There's something else. I feel God is directing me to visit Grandfather Truelove."

"I doubt Daddy would jump on board with that."

"Daddy has to forgive Grandfather. I think God wants us to help him find peace."

"I'll add that to my prayer list," Opie promised.

"Thanks." They heard the bathroom door open. Val grabbed her robe. "Wonder if there's any hot water left."

"Probably not. That's one thing we need to change if we stay here," Opie said.

Later that night, after the house grew silent, Val found herself unable to sleep. She had prayed, thanking God as always and seeking guidance on the family's move. She had also prayed about the situation between her father and grandfather. Thoughts of that led her back to the situation between Russ and Wendell, and she prayed for them, too. He'd really done well with the plans. She thanked God for yet another answered prayer in Russ's excellent design.

That comment about buying a date had certainly backfired on her. She'd only wanted to lighten the mood after telling him about Opie and Wendell. When he'd said that about knowing how to treat a woman she wondered what dating Russ would be like. For years she had waited for God to send the man He intended for her. Could Russ be the one?

Quietly, she slipped out of the bed and

knelt to pray.

God, I don't know what You have in mind, but please guide me through this new venture. Keep my family safe and happy, and shower them with all the blessings You have in store for each of them. Give the graduates clear minds and help them make decisions that will improve their lives. Bless Daddy with the success of this farm and me with my business. And make us all better servants to You.

Eight

"What's the latest on the Truelove project?" Randall King asked the following morning when they met in the hallway.

The desire to keep walking was strong. "A few alterations, but she basically okayed the plans."

His boss smiled. "Excellent. And you recommended Kevin Flint?"

The burning sensation in his stomach increased. "We've got a problem there. I explained that a bigger company could get the job done more quickly, but she insists on giving the job to smaller contractors. She's not budging on that."

"You didn't convince her you made your recommendations based on what's best for the project. Doesn't she trust you?"

He made it sound as if Russ hadn't tried to change Val's mind. Trust had nothing to do with the situation. She viewed this as an opportunity to help the less fortunate. "She has very definite plans for her business," Russ told him. "She's already said she'll find someone else to carry forth the vision if we can't come to an agreement."

"Get her in here and let's discuss this."

"I'll see when she's available. She's very busy."

"We can go there," Randall clipped out. "I want to see what they've done."

Russ didn't like the sound of that. Still, he doubted the man could smooth talk any of the Trueloves. He'd learned the hard way that they knew what they wanted and expected of the people they hired.

"Yes, sir. Is there a time that's better for you?" Russ asked as he led the way into his office. The man pulled out his PDA and listed several appointment times. Russ carefully noted them and promised to get back to him.

Val wouldn't like this, Russ thought. He figured she'd construe it as his effort to coerce her into doing what he'd recommended. That definitely wasn't the case.

As he settled at his desk, Russ wondered why Mr. King insisted Kevin Flint be brought in. He knew the two men were great friends, but Flint Construction had plenty of business already.

Aware Val wouldn't be in the house at this

time of day, he dialed her cell number. As the phone rang, he considered the previous evening. He'd actually enjoyed himself. And while he wouldn't admit it to anyone else, Russ envied the devotion of the Truelove family. In the years since the death of his parents he had felt alone, particularly when he found himself in family settings.

When Val spoke of the monetary gifts she planned for the graduates, he couldn't help but think she'd already given up so much for them. He found it difficult to believe she was willing to give more.

"Hi, it's Russ," he said quickly. "Hope I'm not interrupting."

"I'm due a break."

"Thanks again for dinner. I really enjoyed myself."

"Consider yourself welcome any time."

Taking a deep breath, Russ jumped into the reason for his call. "Mr. King asked me to contact you and set up a time to visit the site."

"Is that the next step once the client approves the plans?"

Russ swallowed, feeling deceitful as he said, "I think he just wants to get an idea of what you have in the works."

"When did you have in mind? Morning is best for me."

"Ten o'clock okay?" Russ asked after double-checking the list.

"Nine would be better," Val said.

"I don't think he has an opening then."

"Ten is fine. Come to the English garden."

"Uh, Val, where is that?"

"Behind the house. Where I was working when you came by with the first set of plans."

"Oh, okay. How did the contractor visit go?"

"Like you thought. We don't have the final figures yet, but he said it would cost a lot to do all we want to do. I talked with Daddy, and we're praying over moving into the big house."

"Hope it works out for you."

"Thanks, Russ. What did you think of Daddy's suggestion that we lower the structure?"

The conversation turned to the pros and cons of changing the plans.

"I'll make those revisions this afternoon and bring the plans out tomorrow. Please thank your parents again for their hospitality."

"I will. See you soon."

Early the following morning Russ found himself in the passenger seat of his employer's expensive sports car. While he enjoyed the luxury of the fine automobile, he dreaded the upcoming meeting.

"You know Ms. Truelove best," Randall King said. "How should we approach her?"

Russ had learned what he knew the hard way, and deep down inside he suspected this visit was a mistake. "Advising fast action is vital for her business, I suppose," he said, hoping that didn't sound too stupid.

Randall glanced at him. "You'd think that would be important. Time and money are key factors in getting any new operation off the ground. Does she strike you as hesitant about this project? Maybe she's in no hurry to see the structure completed?"

"No, sir. She's one hundred percent ready to start. From what she's told me, this has been a longtime dream she had no hope of achieving until she won the money."

"That's incredible luck."

"Luck isn't a word the Trueloves use," Russ told him. "They attribute it to God answering Val's prayers."

Randall glanced at him. "Really?"

"Yes, sir. I wish He'd answer some of mine like that."

"You a praying man, Russ?"

"No, sir," he admitted.

"There are some good connections to be made in church. Lots of networking gets done on Sunday mornings."

He might not be a Christian, but Russ had attended church enough to know that using God's house for anything other than worship wasn't the act of a wise man.

"I spoke with Kevin just this past Sunday about pending projects. He's very interested in this job."

Probably thinks he can gouge Val outrageously, Russ thought.

Randall King slowed and hit the signal as he approached the entrance to Sheridan Farm. Like other farms in the area, a stack stone fence stood there with a plaque indicating the property name. "I haven't been here since Mrs. Sheridan died. The old man didn't entertain after that."

"It's a definite showplace," Russ agreed.

They were surprised when a guard came forward at the closed gate. Russ wondered what had precipitated the need for protection. After giving their names, the man checked his list and directed them through.

"Why do they have security?" Randall asked.

"I don't know. There wasn't anyone here the other night." Russ indicated the area to their right. "Park here. Val said she'd be in the garden behind the house."

As they approached, Russ noted how they

141

had worked to restore the beautiful garden to its former glory. The difference between that first visit and now was incredible.

"Watch your step," Val called when they approached the area where the stones were missing.

"Hello, Ms. Truelove. Good to see you," Randall King said, extending his hand as he moved forward.

Val pulled off her garden gloves and shook his hand. "You, too, Mr. King. Russ."

"You've been busy," Russ commented.

Val nodded and looked back at the expansive area. "I have a wedding and reception scheduled in this garden for August."

"You're already scheduling?"

His boss sounded surprised. "Kelly is having her wedding here," Russ offered, avoiding Val's gaze when he realized she wouldn't like his sharing that information. He looked at her and mouthed, "Sorry."

Val gave him a hopeless shake of her head and turned her attention to Randall King.

"Certainly a beautiful place. I was just telling Russ I attended many parties here before Mrs. Sheridan died."

"She did love to entertain," Val said, remembering the elderly woman fondly. "Would you like a tour? We're concentrating our efforts on the English and Japanese gardens."

They strolled along the paths, discussing the various plants that had begun to bloom. "I adore spring," Val said. "It's so wonderful to see the flowers after the long cold winter."

"The cycle of life," Randall King commented.

Val glanced at Russ. "I asked the contractor to give me quotes on smoke alarms, doors, and emergency lighting for the B and B."

"You found a contractor?" Russ asked.

"Not for the structure."

He almost groaned when she gave Randall King the perfect lead-in. He grabbed the opportunity. "Russ tells me he recommended Kevin Flint's company."

"He did," Val agreed. "And I explained I want to provide the opportunity to a smaller company. I'm sure Mr. Flint does excellent work, but I feel this is a chance to give back to the community."

"But surely you understand we only have your best interests at heart," Randall said. "As a businesswoman, you need the job completed in a timely, efficient manner by someone who knows the ins and outs of construction."

"I do know that," she agreed. "And my plan is to find the contractor who can complete the plan as well as Mr. Flint's company."

As Russ watched the interplay between them, he realized it pleased him she didn't allow the man to intimidate her.

"You realize we cannot recommend these other contractors?"

Appearing somewhat surprised, Val asked, "Does Prestige only do business with one contractor? I would have thought a company your size would have many contacts for their various projects. Giving preferential treatment to one company doesn't strike me as timely or efficient. What happens when Mr. Flint's company has more projects than it can handle at any given time?"

"He hires more crews."

"How can he be aware of what's going on at the different sites?"

"Kevin is the owner," Randall said. "He has site foremen who report back to him."

"I suppose that's an okay way to do business, but I want to be more involved in the process. I plan to know exactly what's going on with my business at any given time."

Randall looked skeptical. "While I appreciate the motivation behind that at startup, you will find that as the business grows you'll be forced to depend on others

to keep you apprised of day-to-day opera-
tions."

"I don't think you believe that," Val told
him. "You gave this assignment to Russ, and
yet your presence here indicates a personal
involvement on your part."

Good one, Russ thought, glancing over to
find his boss's expression growing tighter
by the minute.

"I'm sure Russ told you we approved the
plans night before last," Val said. "I'm eager
to get started. Would you like to see the
site?"

"Certainly."

Russ groaned inwardly at the thought of
the jeep and his boss's expensive suit. Relief
filled him when today's vehicle of choice
was a golf cart. He wondered why she'd
stuck him in that old jeep as he settled in
the back, leaving the front passenger seat
for his employer.

"Will you get the gate?" she asked Randall
King a couple of minutes later.

"I've got it." Russ jumped out and ran to
release the latch, reversing the process after
Val drove through.

"Good view," Randall commented when
she pulled up before the vista.

"God truly had a red-letter day when He
created the Kentucky bluegrass region."

"Spoken like a true Kentuckian."

"Imagine this venue with all the accoutrements of romance — a beautiful structure, happy guests, moonlight, stars, and abiding love."

"You evoke many possibilities in my mind," Randall said.

Russ doubted the man had any romantic thoughts beyond the dollars and cents of business.

"I hope to evoke more than a few memories over the years," Val agreed. "Our intent is that Your Wedding Place becomes the premier venue for weddings within Kentucky and maybe an even broader appeal to the bridal community. Before we're finished I'd love to hear Your Wedding Place become a name on every bride's lips."

Randall King nodded. "Given your funds, you can do whatever you want. Why weddings?"

"The money is a blessing," Val agreed. "We've been able to make decisions that will affect the future of every member of the family. But none of us believes God provided the money to be wasted. I'm hoping this business will secure my future. In turn, each of my siblings will do the same with their plans."

"And if this fails?"

"We put our faith in God and trust Him for our success," Val said confidently.

Randall nodded as he glanced at his watch. "Regretfully, I must get back to the office for a lunch meeting. I hope to see more as things develop."

Val flashed him a brilliant smile. "Who knows? Perhaps you'll even avail yourself of our services one day."

"Perhaps I will."

Russ felt a surge of jealousy as he watched Randall King flirt with Val. The man had already left one wife behind, and if the rumors were true, he dabbled with the affections of a great number of other women. He should warn Val to steer clear.

She parked the cart near the sports car, and after Randall King climbed out she looked at Russ and whispered, "We need to talk."

He'd known this was coming and could tell from her tone she wasn't pleased. "I'll call you later."

"Do that."

"Ready, Russ?"

"Yes, sir."

"It's been a pleasure, Ms. Truelove."

"Please call me Val."

"Only if you call me Randall. I hope you will reconsider allowing Kevin Flint to build your structure. You'll find him very reliable."

"I'm sorry, but no. I know I can find a suitable contractor who deserves a chance."

"Full of herself, isn't she?" Randall King said minutes later as they drove off the property.

"She knows what she wants."

"Does she?" he inquired blandly. "She's a little girl playing grownup in the real world. I don't think she truly has a clue about what lies ahead for her."

"What do you mean?"

"Let's just say she's not chosen an easy path. That type of business comes and goes. There's no security. But I suppose with her funds she can keep trying until she gets it right."

"I think she has a good idea," Russ said.

"You're here to do a job. And I suggest you complete it as quickly as possible," Randall suggested. "Prestige has other clients we need to focus on."

The man's attitude seemed to sour more with each word. She'd really upset the big boss, Russ thought. "I told you she has very definite ideas about what she wants."

Randall's piercing gaze focused on him, his words accusatory when he spoke. "But you allowed me to waste my time?"

Russ resented Randall King's attempt to

turn the situation on him. "I'm sorry, sir, but I did warn you."

"You did nothing to support me in convincing her to change her mind."

Russ closed his eyes, holding back the sigh that threatened to escape. "I've tried. I hoped that hearing it from you would make her rethink the situation."

"I don't expect you to give up. I want Kevin Flint on that job."

Russ didn't understand his insistence.

"When you hire Prestige Designs, you receive the benefit of my years of experience. Can you believe she actually thinks she's going to be hands-on with every aspect of her business? She's a lamb in a world of wolves."

After watching the two of them earlier, Russ thought Val could hold her own with any wolf. He listened to Randall King vent throughout the remainder of the drive and was glad when his boss pulled into his parking space at the office. "Wrap up the plans for the Truelove project and move on," he ordered as they entered the building.

Russ wanted to argue there was considerable work to be completed but decided it best to keep quiet for now.

Randall King stomped off, and Russ felt overwhelming dread. He told Cheryl he was going to lunch and checked to make sure he had his cell so he could stop along the way and call Val. Gut instinct warned him not to call from the office. Once in his car, he dialed and waited for an answer.

"What was that visit about this morning?" she demanded without greeting. "Your boss may be big on Kevin Flint, but I've heard things about him and his company and don't care to become involved. I'm beginning to wonder if I made a mistake by choosing Prestige Designs."

"I'm sorry we blindsided you." Russ meant that. In the past he'd probably have shrugged and gone on with his business; but he liked Val, and now that they had sorted out the plans he looked forward to working with her. If Mr. King allowed him to continue, Russ thought. "I should have warned you when I called, but please understand I'm in a precarious position. I'm close to completing my internship at Prestige. Once I pass my exam it will be different. I can't jeopardize all my hard work."

"Common courtesy would have been a heads-up that he was gunning for me to hire his contractor," Val said, sounding none too happy.

Between these two he couldn't win. "I get

the point. He's not very happy right now, either."

"Do I need to take my plans and move on?"

"I wish you wouldn't," Russ said. "As I told you before this is a first in my career, and I'd like to see it completed."

She remained silent for a few seconds longer. "I don't like being played."

"I tried to tell him, but he felt we could talk you into changing your mind."

"And you agreed he should try?"

"What choice did I have, Val?" Russ asked, his ire rising. "The man is my boss."

"You already pointed that out, but I'd like to believe you feel some loyalty toward your clients as well."

"What would you have done? You worked for Maddy. I'm sure there were times when she wanted you to do things you didn't necessarily agree with. Did you tell her no?"

"I understand what you're up against, but I don't like being challenged either. It's important I carry through on my plans with or without Prestige. Why does he want Kevin Flint involved anyway? I'd think the two of them would have bigger projects to pursue."

Russ agreed with her. "I don't know."

"I'll give you the benefit of the doubt, but

please don't allow this to happen again. Company loyalty aside, you need to understand I won't tolerate deception."

"When did you get the security guard?" Russ asked, hoping to change the subject.

"Today." She told him about Derrick's visit. "Daddy wants me to hire a driver."

"Other farms have their own police forces to protect the horses. Don't you consider yourself as important as any horse?"

"I'm not interested in being followed around."

"But you realize it's a practical consideration."

"I suppose so," Val said. "For all of us. Anyone who wanted to get to me could easily do it through any member of my family. They're going to be upset."

"But safe, and that's all that matters. Hey, the garden looks great. You'll be ready for the wedding soon."

"That brings me to another subject."

"I know. Kelly's wedding. It just slipped out."

"What if she doesn't plan to invite him?"

"She already has. He won't come though. He'll offer his regrets and send a gift. He doesn't socialize with the lower ranks of his staff."

"I don't care for your involvement in my

business. Having access to information involving Your Wedding Place does not give you the right to apprise others of my plans."

Russ couldn't help himself. "Well, truthfully I didn't get the information from you. Kelly told me. So basically, I shared what she told me."

Val's heavy sigh reached across the miles. "Just finish the plans, Russ. I have a few contractors lined up to come and look over the job. I want to get this in the works quickly."

They had left the farm barely an hour ago. "Where did you find contractors?" he asked curiously.

"I figured I'd better find someone if I didn't want Kevin Flint shoved down my throat. A couple of companies in Lexington showed an interest."

"When are you meeting with them? I need to be in on the discussions."

Val gave him the appointment times and wrapped up the conversation with a warning reminder that she didn't expect any more surprises.

NINE

Maddy brought her bride out on Saturday morning, and the woman fell in love with the Japanese garden.

"It will be even better by your wedding day," Val promised.

"I can't imagine that," Leah Bainbridge said, looking around at the perfect arrangement of water, stones, and greenery. "Do you live in the house?"

Val shook her head. "My family lives elsewhere on the property."

When the woman looked surprised, Val fought back the temptation to explain the recent acquisition. She'd learned the less said, the better.

"And this garden is available on the fourth Saturday in August?"

"It is. We've only recently begun booking weddings. You're our second bride."

"Second? I don't —"

Maddy interceded quickly. "Val worked as

my assistant for years. She knows the business inside and out. In fact, I depended on her to procure the best venues. She does a masterful job. I'm so thankful she's started this business."

"Your Wedding Place will do everything possible to fulfill your needs," Val assured her.

Leah nodded. "Is it possible to have the reception here as well?"

"We could set up tables and chairs around the area after the ceremony. Or, we plan to bring in a large tent for a wedding the weekend before yours. We could make that available for your use."

The woman looked at Maddy.

"The tent sounds like a perfect solution. We'll discuss it further and get back to you."

"I'll e-mail you the cost sheets," Val said.

After the women left, Val felt a huge sense of accomplishment. She hadn't even opened for business and already had two bookings. That certainly boded well for the future. The desire to share the news with someone was strong. Opie had left for New York that morning, and her mother had gone with Heath and Jane to run errands after driving her to the airport. Without thinking, she dialed Russ's number.

"Hi. I just booked my second wedding.

It's the week after Kelly's, but we'll be able to use the tent set up for both weddings. I'm so happy."

"I can tell," Russ said. "Hang on."

She listened to the music for a couple of minutes before he returned. "Sorry. I had a client on the other line."

"I caught you at a bad time. I'll let you —"

"It's okay," Russ said. "I have to get some information together and call back. Would you like to go out tonight and celebrate?"

"Yes," she said without hesitation.

An unfamiliar feeling of anticipation filled Val that night as she walked into the living room to await Russ's arrival. She'd found herself going back and forth ever since she'd said yes, wondering if she'd made the right decision.

She wore one of the sundresses she'd bought on the recent shopping trip along with a pair of sandals. Her freshly washed hair hung down her back.

When Russ rang the bell she greeted him and accepted the bouquet of spring flowers he offered. "I should have done this when Kelly booked."

"Before or after I bit your head off for telling her my business plans?" Val asked with a grin.

"Maybe before if I'd been faster on the draw," Russ countered with an easy smile.

He drove to the French restaurant Kelly had recommended in downtown Paris. The warm atmosphere of the old commercial building was evidently popular with the locals. After noting the way people stared and whispered, he said, "I'm sorry. It didn't occur to me people would act this way. I suppose it has to do with your recent celebrity status. Becoming rich overnight is a major accomplishment."

"I certainly don't want a lottery win to become my biggest achievement in life," Val said. "And I wouldn't mind people treating me like they did before the money."

Russ seated her in the chair that put her back to the group. "Would you give the money back if you had to decide again?"

"Maybe. At least on some days. I was so unprepared for instant wealth. People believe they can handle it, but I can list two negatives for every positive." She sighed. "I always said I wanted to get to the point where a hundred dollars wasn't a lot of money."

Russ grinned. "You're definitely past that."

Val shook her head. "No. It's still a lot of money. I've made a couple of spur-of-the-moment decisions I don't regret, but managing this much money isn't as easy as people think. Every decision involves a great deal of prayer. Daddy's managed Sheridan Farm for years, but even he agrees there's an unexpected level of responsibility that comes with ownership. Basically, we handed the controls over to God and listen when He tells us what to do."

"I'm sure it'll get easier with time." After Russ ordered an appetizer of calamari, he lifted his water glass in a toast.

"I'm so happy. I can't help but hope this is a hint of what's to come."

"You say Maddy referred this bride?"

"She's agreed to recommend Your Wedding Place. I need to contact other planners and get the interest going there as well."

"You should have a launch party. Allow the planners to stroll the gardens."

Val liked the idea. "We could do tours and pass out literature. Opie could handle the refreshments."

"What happened to keeping a low profile?"

"It occurred to me that publicizing Your Wedding Place gives it a stronger foundation than secrecy. If someone steals the idea in my head, I can't argue the point. If people are aware it's my business, I stand a better chance. I considered franchising."

Russ let out a low whistle. "That's expensive."

"And it might make sense if the venue idea caught on, but given the cost I decided to invest the money back into my business."

"Give them what they want so they'll come?"

"I hope so."

After they placed their orders for the house special chicken, Russ suggested, "Let's talk about something other than work."

"Like what?" Val asked.

"Tell me about you," Russ invited.

"Not much you don't already know. I was born in Kentucky and basically grew up here in Paris as the oldest of seven."

"What's that like?"

"You're never alone," Val offered with a tongue-in-cheek grin. "You've witnessed it for yourself a couple of times."

"You never wanted to break away from the family?"

"No. I like having them around. I'm glad Opie and the twins are back. I missed them."

"Do you want a large family?" Russ asked.

"I'll take what God gives me. I've always thought three kids would be good."

"Why three?"

"I feel sorry for that half kid in the averages," she said, grinning at Russ's surprised expression. "I figure if I take my half kid and someone else's, we can get a whole kid into the world." She broke into laughter. "Just kidding, Russ." The irony struck her, and Val laughed harder. "Kidding," she repeated. "I'm sorry. Guess you have to be there," she said, wiping her eyes carefully so she didn't smear her eyeliner.

Russ laughed at her fit of giggles. "It's a good number. I know what you mean about the age gaps. There are five years between Wendell and me."

"Your mom must have been surprised when you came along."

"Wendell's mom died when he was three. Our dad married my mother a year later. Then he went away to school not long after I was born. We never had much of a relationship."

"You didn't attend school here?"

"Dad sent us to boarding school. I spent very little time in Kentucky after that."

Russ's life struck Val as sad. He'd spent his formative years under the guidance of others. When he could have forged a deeper relationship with his family, his parents had died. Their loss had resulted in the estrangement over the farm that destroyed any hope of Russ's forming a relationship with his brother.

"It's not as if you can't afford your own place," Russ said, taking the conversation back to her.

"I could." Val's shoulders lifted in a tiny shrug. "If I decided that's what I want. I need to remain close to the farm since my business is there."

"Yet another reason to live in the Sheridans' house. It's more than large enough to hold all of you."

"We're looking at options. If I convert to a B and B, I'd have to live there when guests are in the house. If I rent to overnight parties, they wouldn't want me around."

"That house is much too valuable to rent out like a hotel room," Russ objected. "People are too careless of other people's things."

"Things could happen even if I lived there. We're back to business," Val pointed out. "Your turn. Where do you live?"

"I have a two-bedroom, two-and-a-half-bath condo in Lexington. I considered renting, but the condo was the better investment."

"And it's yours, and you can make changes if you want," Val said.

Russ's smile told her he got her point.

"And if I respond to that we're back to discussing business."

"Yes," Val agreed, "but then business is key to our relationship, don't you think? You invited me to dinner to celebrate my latest success."

"The most recent of many," Russ pronounced.

"I pray that's the case. I do like your idea of a launch party. In fact, I can hardly wait to start planning."

"You really want this, don't you?"

Val felt self-conscious as she noted the way he studied her. "More than you can imagine. Did you ever dream of something you knew you'd never get to do?"

Russ nodded. "My dream seemed more achievable in my youth when I thought I'd inherit a portion of the farm. I honestly believed I could have it all."

"You could still own a farm," Val said. "Perhaps not as grand as Hunter Farm, but there are other acreages available."

"And you could have had your business," Russ said. "Not as a site provider but a procurer."

"So we've limited our visions?" Val asked. "I suppose I could have found a way, but it always seemed impossible. Now that everything is unfolding, I feel God has worked the most incredible miracle in my life."

Russ took a sip of his water. "You talk about God a lot."

"He's important to me. I'm nothing without Him," Val said simply.

Russ's puzzlement forced her to explain.

"I can't take full credit for my accomplishments," Val said. "It isn't anything I do. God knows the plans He has for me. Yet He gave me freedom to make choices and even knows the choices I'll make."

Russ frowned and shook his head. "I doubt God has time to worry about me."

"Why do you doubt Him? He cares about His lambs."

Her words reminded Russ of Randall King's comment about Val being a lamb in a world of wolves. "I've never been referred to as a lamb before."

"Come to church with me," Val invited impulsively. "You're an educated, informed man. Don't you think it's fair to give God a chance before making the decision not to follow Him?"

The way Russ concentrated on the food, placing his knife and fork just so, folding his napkin and doing everything but look at her, provided her answer. Seeing his discomfort, Val retreated. "This meal is really delicious."

"Not as good as your mother's," Russ said.

"Mom's adapting to Opie wanting to try different techniques with her basic meat-and-potatoes foods."

"They're excellent cooks."

Val smiled. "If I tell them that, you'll have a standing invitation for dinner."

"I wouldn't mind that."

"There's always room for one more around the Truelove dining table."

They finished their meal and opted for coffee instead of dessert. "I really appreciate your celebrating with me," she said as she stirred sugar into her cup.

"I'm happy for you, Val. I don't think I realized how much all this meant to you until tonight. I look forward to playing my part in seeing your dreams fulfilled."

"Thanks, Russ. I need all the help I can get."

"Oh, I'm beginning to see you as a mover and shaker in this world."

"That might not be a good thing."

"Whatever it is, I'm happy to be part of your successes."

Ten

With August drawing near, the pace picked up around the Truelove home. From the time the younger kids wrapped up their school year in early June, they jumped in to help wherever they could. The days of summer rolled forward as they all worked toward a shared goal, and together they had made great strides with the gardens.

She and Heath had talked, and she agreed he should do what he wanted. She even paid him a salary, insisting she'd do the same if she hired someone for the job. Opie had done some stints as a private chef and helped when she had free time. She continued to review her options and assisted their mother in preparing family meals and taking care of the house.

Rom accepted the Lexington job. When he asked for apartment leads, Russ offered his guest room for as long as Rom needed. Russ and the twins shared many common interests and often did things together.

Jane added joy to every activity with her laughter and teasing. Val couldn't help but smile as she considered the conversation they'd had earlier when she asked how Jane felt about antiques.

"I suppose they're the distant cousins to my decorating style. Early castoffs."

Val explained her plan. Antique shops filled downtown Paris, and she hoped to replace the pieces the Sheridans' son had taken from the house.

"I'll try anything once," Jane said. "You should know I know nothing about antiques."

"Me either. I think it might be fun to see what we can find. I particularly want to retain the authenticity in the first-floor rooms."

Jane had agreed, and Val planned to set a time for their antique hunting.

Jane and Sammy were a good fit to their family. From the moment she'd laid eyes on Sammy, their mom had fallen in love with her, and the toddler spent most of her days playing with Cindy Truelove nearby. When Jane asked if it was too much, Val's mom told her she'd missed having small children around the house.

Val knew her mother wanted grandchildren; and while being married and having a family had always seemed to be one of her more achievable dreams, here she was single with her business capturing first place. Life certainly had taken a full turn.

Her prayers that the Lord would guide her to the right man remained unanswered. Nevertheless, when she found Russ playing around in her thoughts more often, Val didn't know what to think. She liked him a lot, but the fact that he didn't have a relationship with Jesus Christ made her think twice about getting involved with him.

They had interviewed a number of contractors and found one that could handle the project. Todd Bigelow's company might not be the largest in Lexington, but after talking with him Val knew he was the best man for the job. A believer like her, he felt led of God to do the best possible job for every client. She knew he would have said no if he didn't feel he could handle the work.

Russ called late one afternoon and suggested they get together to discuss the project. Tired after a busy day, she had refused but then relented when he insisted it was important they talk. That evening, he visited with her family while he waited for her.

"You look nice," he said, rising to his feet when she entered the room.

"Thanks."

He took her hand, calling good night to the others before they walked out to his newer model sports car.

Russ drove to his favorite Lexington restaurant, an out-of-the-way place he said would give them anonymity. They followed their waitress through the cozy old building to a table near the window facing the street. After studying the menu Val ordered grilled pork chops, and he opted for fried chicken, both with a variety of vegetables. The scents from the pie store next door nearly drove them crazy.

"I'm not leaving here without dessert," Russ said.

"Maybe we should just skip dinner and go straight for the pies."

"What would your mother think?" he teased. "Okay, so what's your choice? Colonnade or pavilion? You need to decide so I can order the trim."

"The house is colonial, and I love the columns; but I'm not sure I want a big Greek-style structure out there," Val said. "I saw something the other day with a wrought-iron top I really liked. Still, I don't want the brides thinking we've created a folly and saying no thanks to that either."

When reviewing the various structures, she'd learned a folly was a building considered strictly as a decoration. She had no place in her project for something like that.

"If you make the other structure an enclosed fabric-covered building, you don't really want canopies here, do you?" Russ asked.

"Yes and no. I like the idea of being open to the sky, but some brides will want protection for their guests. Could we do the wrought iron with rods underneath so we can connect shade fabric if requested?"

He found an envelope in his pocket and quickly sketched swirls and twirls into a design for the iron. "What about this? Panels domed over the top of the structure."

"How would they be supported?"

"We could bring the wrought iron down support posts. Or use arches."

"The arches could be placed to mimic windows," Val said thoughtfully.

"So it's going to be a pavilion?"

Val felt torn. The right look was crucial. "I don't know. What do you think?"

"Black wrought iron would probably suit the area best."

"Then let's make it a pavilion."

"Mr. King is pushing me to wrap up your

project."

Val appreciated his candor. "You think it's because I wouldn't choose his contractor?"

"I have no idea, but I plan to keep working with you until the job is completed."

"Aren't you afraid you'll get into trouble with your boss?"

"I understand why that might be a concern for you, but I promise not to compromise the project for fear of losing my job."

"We'll work it out," Val said.

She had believed they could — until Todd called to say the plans had not been approved because of missing documents. Val wanted to scream. With the demands of two weddings and the launch party, she didn't need this. After taking a few minutes to pray over the situation, she dialed Russ's cell phone.

"Hi. What's up?"

"Nothing, thanks to you," she ground out angrily.

"What do you mean?"

Val knew she needed to calm down. "Todd checked online to see if the plans were approved, and evidently they were rejected because they were incomplete. When did you plan to let me know?"

"Why didn't he call me?"

No doubt that's what Kevin Flint would have done, Val thought. "Because he wants to start work for *me*," she stressed, "and can't seem to get a permit. You need to sort this out. I don't want to lose this contractor, and we don't need any more holdups."

Thus far they had dealt with problem after problem. The initial plan creation had taken longer than expected, and then Prestige had delivered the package to the wrong review board. Now there was no permit. Val couldn't help but wonder what was going on.

Russ called back an hour later to say everything was under control. "I know those documents were in the plans I gave Mr. King."

"Why would you give them to him?"

"Because that's the way he does business," Russ told her. "He delivers them personally to the planning office."

"The wrong planning office," Val emphasized. "I hope this gets resolved quickly. Todd's eager to start construction, but he can't wait forever for permits."

"I'm on it."

"Times like these make even the pitiful offers like that one from KFD Corporation look good."

"Who?" Russ asked.

"I have no idea who they are. I received a special delivery letter with a post office box in Lexington. I had Mr. Henderson reject the offer."

"Why haven't you mentioned this before?"

"Because selling the farm isn't a consideration," Val admitted, suddenly shamed by her fit of pique. When would she learn to stop reacting?

"I don't understand. Why would they make an offer when you've just bought the place?"

"I have no idea. Sheridan Farm isn't for sale at any price."

After they hung up, Val still felt ill at ease about the situation. What had happened? Had Russ intentionally delayed the project? He seemed to have corrected the problem easily enough.

She didn't want to doubt Russ, and yet she couldn't help but feel something wasn't right. He knew how important this was to her. Even his guarantees didn't make Val feel reassured. She wondered exactly what had happened. Russ had been so confident the information was there, but it was possible he had made a mistake.

Val bowed her head in prayer, beseeching the Lord to bless her project. Pulling her work gloves on, she found Heath placing koi fish in the pond in the Japanese garden. She shared the news with him. "I don't understand these delays."

"I'm sure this type of thing happens all the time, Val."

"Maybe, but Russ said Randall King delivered the information. Wouldn't he check to be sure everything was there?"

Heath reached for another container. "Not if he assumed Russ had done his job. Do you honestly believe Russ would harm your project?"

The thought made her feel sick to her stomach. "I don't want to, Heath, but I can't help but remember that first meeting. He got so upset that he allowed his personal feelings to overwhelm his professional opinion. What if deep down inside he still feels that way?"

"I don't think that's the case. He created an acceptable set of plans and has stuck it out despite his boss's orders to move on."

"More than acceptable," Val agreed. "As I said, I don't know why it bothers me."

"Maybe because you like Russ and don't want to have doubts about him."

She did, and yet Val accepted they were different on too many levels. She suspected involving herself with Russ would be relationship suicide. "He is a nice guy. I like working with him."

"I suspect it's more than that," Heath said.

"No matter how good a friend Russ is, there can't be more," Val said.

"Because he's not a Christian," Heath said. "It's too bad. He has a solid future ahead of him, and I don't think you'd have to be concerned he's after your money."

The Truelove children had the best role models in two Christian parents. They had witnessed firsthand what it took to have a harmonious life and to live in one accord with God.

"Only one thing is certain, Val. God is in control."

"He is, and I'm so very thankful for that."

Russ couldn't get the Truelove project off his mind. How had that document gone missing? He was positive it had been there when he double-checked the plans before handing them over. Val probably thought he'd done this on purpose. Luckily enough it had been resolved, but he would pay closer attention and make sure nothing else happened.

He glanced down at the notes he'd doodled while talking with Val. Who was this KFD Corporation that had made the offer for the farm? Something about the situation bugged him, and he made a mental note to follow up.

He needed to talk with Val. Make her understand. It seemed strange to think he'd been working with her for so long now. They'd come a long way from their first meeting.

At first he'd wondered why her every conversation seemed to come back to the same subject — God. He'd attended church as a kid, but now something better always seemed to crop up on Sundays, whether he was hung over from a late night or wanted to golf or sleep in.

He thought about Val's carefully crafted question and wondered why she equated intelligence to serving God. The bad things that had happened to him weren't exactly what he'd expect from a loving God. Still, Russ had learned to respect Val and her family and their desire to do the right things in life. They'd opened his eyes to why certain things mattered to people who followed God.

He hadn't taken Val up on her invitation to attend church, but he'd awakened early on a couple of Sunday mornings and found himself wondering if he'd get anything out of the experience. Maybe he'd attend after Kelly got back from her honeymoon. That way he'd know someone other than the Trueloves.

The week preceding Kelly Dickerson's wedding had them all working overtime. Val verified the delivery of the tables and chairs and the tent setup, and later worked with Heath replacing the flowers in the planters as requested by the bride.

"We probably should consider using containers that can be lifted in and out easily," Heath said. "I think a greenhouse might be a good addition to the plan. We could grow some things ourselves."

"And break the heart of many a businessman in Paris. We've invested heavily in their profit margins thus far."

On Thursday and Friday Val worked with Kelly, her family, and the wedding planner, making the site everything the young woman wanted. Saturday dawned bright and clear. Val made herself accessible to Kelly and offered rooms in the house for the bride and for her attendants to dress for the event.

She glanced at Heath. "You'd better get dressed if you plan to attend the wedding. Is Rom coming?"

Heath, Rom, and Jane had been part of Kelly's graduating class, and she had invited them to her wedding.

"I don't think so, but Jane and I will be there."

After he'd gone, Val wandered into the garden for one last look around. She found herself looking at the area as a bride would. Yes, she could appreciate this venue for her wedding, though she preferred the view from the new structure. She followed the path to the huge white tent the rental company had erected.

"How's it going?" Russ asked, catching her by surprise.

"You're early." He looked very handsome in his formal wear.

"Thought I'd check in and see if you needed help."

They remained outside the tent. "We're good. Kelly's dressing. The garden is beautiful. I'd give you a peek, but that wouldn't be fair to her."

"I'm sure everyone will be impressed." He looked around. "I never realized how big these things were."

She frowned. "I need my structure completed. Tents are expensive. I should probably invest in one."

"You'd have to hire people to put it up," he said.

"True. But even so I hope there will be more than a few tent rentals before the pavilion is completed."

"Are we okay over the permit problem?"

Val noticed he watched her closely. "I suppose. Todd started work."

"They're excavating the area?"

She nodded. "Daddy and Heath took some of the guys and went in to restructure the fence to make the work area more accessible. They brought in some big equipment."

"Any regrets over seeing your beautiful area dismantled?"

"Not when I know what's going to be there in the end."

"I'm eager to see the end result myself. Though I will say I'm impressed with what I'm seeing already."

"Thanks. Kelly is pleased. It's an honor to know I've played a part in her happy day."

"It's just beginning, Val."

"I pray Your Wedding Place is a success."

"Sheridan Farm will be here no matter what."

"So you do think the business won't survive," she challenged.

"Stop putting words into my mouth. I knew you were still angry."

"I don't understand, Russ," she admitted. "I paid good money to ensure everything moved forward without delay, and we've had nothing but problems."

"I can't explain what happened. I'd swear on my life the information was there when I turned the papers over to Randall King."

"Don't do that," Val chided.

"I didn't do anything to hold up your project," he insisted.

"I want to believe you're with me in this."

He stepped closer, taking her hands in his. Their gazes locked. "I am fully committed to your success. Please believe that." He squeezed her hands gently. "I promise I'm going to see this through to the end. I'll be right here with you all the way."

Electricity charged the air as neither of them moved. Finally Val said, "I'm glad. I need to finish up a couple of things before I turn it over to Kelly."

"She's talked about getting married here ever since she booked."

"She told me. I gave her a special discount for being my first bride. And she's agreed to allow my photographer to take a few photos for publicity purposes."

"You're on your way," Russ said, leaning to kiss her gently before he released her hands. "No more problems," he promised.

He'd surprised her with the kiss, but his own inner turmoil surprised Russ. He'd never felt this way when he'd kissed other women.

Russ hoped he could keep his promises. He recalled the conversation he'd overheard when leaving the office last night. He'd slowed his step when he heard Randall King's comment. Russ knew he shouldn't have eavesdropped but couldn't help himself.

"I know you wanted that property, but she's determined to turn it into something to serve a few brides."

Russ wondered who was on the other end of the line.

"Yes, we could have offered more for the acreage, but we wouldn't have had to if Sheridan hadn't dumped the property so fast." More silence and then Randall King's laughter. "Yeah, I heard that rumor. Even if the old man did hold him in high esteem, it's not likely he'd have instructed his son to give the farm away if he decided to sell."

More silence. "Give her time. It'll get old, and then we can buy the farm for a song. I need to get moving. Dinah promised me a romantic dinner tonight." The man's almost evil laugh gave Russ the creeps.

He knew he should tell Val, but fear silenced his tongue. He'd come too far with Prestige Designs to jeopardize himself at

180

this stage in the process. He had delayed his career for a few years after college while he rebelled out of hurt. When he'd found no peace in his actions, he'd vowed to show them all. Becoming a successful architect in his own right would prove he needed no one but himself.

Still, Russ promised to keep his eyes and ears open. He'd meant it when he said he was with her all the way. No one was going to hurt Val. He'd do everything humanly possible to protect Val and her family.

ELEVEN

Val felt a great deal of satisfaction as she glanced around the area. With Jane's help, she had contacted every wedding planner within miles of Paris and invited him or her to the launch party.

The roses were in full bloom, and she looked forward to welcoming everyone to see their beauty. The theme was a Summer Rose Tea Party, and they had invited the attendees to wear the pastels of a summer bouquet, including hats or parasols. Pastel cloths draped the tables, and real English bone china teacups and silver teapots added the perfect final touch. She had even found a rose paperweight for each guest and had them engraved with Your Wedding Place's name, phone number and Web site.

Euphoria from the success of Kelly's wedding had carried Val through the last four days. Having the two weddings on connecting weeks along with her event enabled her to split the tent rental three ways. She scheduled her event for Thursday afternoon and opted to serve refreshments there rather than in the house. Opie had prepared a true English tea with scones, savories, and a multitude of other items.

The ad agency had used some of Val's photographs to create the banners that hung from the walls of the tent. Large prints of the structure and the plans stood on easels behind a small replica of the pavilion Russ had created for her. They had made the right decision with the wrought-iron top. He'd incorporated ribbons in part of the design to show the option of shade fabric.

"It's fantastic," Jane declared as she set the vase of pastel roses on the table. "I'd book my wedding today," she declared. "Well, if I were getting married."

Val smiled. "I know God has a Mr. Right who will love you and Sammy as you deserve to be loved."

She noted the way Jane's gaze moved across the room to where Heath worked.

"I hope so. I'd like for Sammy to have a man in her life."

"What about Jane?" Val asked.

Her friend grinned. "She could use one in her life, too."

Val picked up rose petals and pushed a

rose further into the container. "I've been thinking." Jane groaned playfully. "No seriously," she said. "We could host an annual event for brides and couples. Show them what we have to offer."

"You could rent space to planners and other service providers to help offset the cost."

"Maybe even give a wedding venue as a door prize."

"We haven't even gotten through our second event, and you're already planning for more."

"Advertising has resulted in a number of calls from brides. I had a couple inquire about spending their wedding night in the house last week."

"What have you decided?"

"We'll be moving into the Sheridan house. Only the grand staircase and drawing room will be available for weddings."

"I'm glad. It's such a beautiful house."

Val agreed. She'd always loved the Sheridan home, and knowing her family would live there made her feel blessed beyond compare. The decision had not been easy. They had prayed about it and had a few family discussions over whether it was the best move. Understandably, her parents had the most ties to the old house where they had raised their family, but they'd agreed the extra space would be nice. They even understood why she wanted to share the home with them. "I know we'll be happy there."

The event had been a big success. The planners loved the theme. Many of them wore hats Val felt certain they'd purchased for Derby parties. Val blushed when Maddy told them she'd lost her star assistant but gained a wonderful new vendor. The one negative had been Derrick's arrival with his new boss.

"You can't keep a good man down," he sniped when Val welcomed them to the event. She managed a smile, all the while praying Derrick didn't cause a scene.

"Val and I worked together in our former lives," she overheard him telling one of the other planners. "She really lucked out when Maddy gave her that winning lottery ticket."

"I see Derrick's already hard at work, doing what he does best," Maddy commented when she walked over to where Val stood.

"Making me miserable?" Val guessed. "I wish he'd never found out about the money."

Maddy grinned. "Hard to keep something like that a secret."

"I know, but this event has to do with my business."

Maddy shrugged. "So tell them the money's an answer to a prayer and launch into the Your Wedding Place spiel. Then have your waitstaff inundate Derrick with refreshments. Maybe that will shut his mouth."

"Hmm, that's an idea. Where's Opie?" Val asked, glancing around for her sister. "She can talk food ad nauseum. With any luck she'd drive him out of here in a few minutes."

Maddy laughed. "You can do this, Val. Remember the time you talked that bride into having her wedding at the Cane Ridge Meeting House?"

"She wanted an old church."

The Cane Ridge Meeting House was just east of Paris and built in 1791. The church had hosted one of the largest camp meetings on the frontier in 1801. Between twenty thousand and thirty thousand people had brought their livestock and spent six days worshipping the Lord. Today a superstructure housed the old restored church which could be used for special occasions.

"And you pleased her with the suggestion. It's a great party, Val. The setup is perfect. People are raving over everything. I'm sure you'll have plenty of interested planners. Now get out there and network." Her former employer gave her a little nudge.

"Thanks, Maddy."

Val noted that Derrick kept his distance, but his in-your-face attitude bothered her a great deal. She asked God's protection and felt happy when he left the party early.

Russ showed up a few minutes later.

Val looped her arm through his. "I'm glad you could come."

He glanced around. "Good turnout."

"The planners are very receptive," Val told him.

"Looks like we'll have to go out and celebrate again."

"This one's on me." A group beckoned her over, and she said, "Visit the refreshment table. Opie outdid herself."

He watched as Val greeted her guests and talked exuberantly about her new business venture. Russ couldn't help but be impressed by what he'd seen. No doubt a number of brides would enjoy their weddings all the more because of Val's business. She had a good idea. He'd done a bit of research and been surprised by the amount of money being spent on weddings.

Russ spotted Opie when he neared the

food table. "Your sister has been bragging about you."

Opie smiled. "She's doing incredibly, don't you think?"

"Val always impresses me."

"Really?"

"Don't get that look in your eye," he warned. "We're friends."

"Lots of couples have started with much less."

Russ considered Opie's comment as he filled his plate and found an out-of-the-way place to sit. He did admire Val and found her attractive. He also knew Val would expect things of the man in her life that he wasn't certain he was prepared to give.

How would a man deal with all that money? Not that he had minded helping spend a bit of it with the project, but Russ didn't care for the idea of being kept by his wife. Their dad had taught his sons that a man's role in the family was provider. Russ didn't plan to settle for less. When it came to his wife and kids, he would be the breadwinner. Still, he couldn't help but consider the possibility of having Val in his life.

"Hi. Val tells us you can answer any questions we might have."

Russ glanced up at the two women standing there and swallowed hastily. He wiped his mouth and spent the next few minutes talking with the planners.

"And when do you project it will be ready?"

"Definitely before spring."

"Val certainly has a good idea," one of the women declared.

"I know Maddy hates that she gave her that ticket," the other one said.

Feeling protective, Russ said, "I'm sure Val will be happy to help you ladies with bookings if you're interested."

"And what did you say this — ?"

"The pavilion will be the ultimate reception site. The upper floor has a breathtaking view of the pastoral rolling hills of Kentucky. We're keeping the structure low to the ground with steps that lead to terraces with seating, fountains, and beautiful landscaping. The underground room is well lit and not the least confining. The upper structure will be open-air. Val tells me brides will fall in love all over again while they share their day with their guests. You should come back once we get closer to completion. The view goes on for miles."

"Did Russ answer your questions, ladies?" Val asked as she joined the group.

"He did. We can't wait to see the area. It

sounds spectacular. You should have another party to show it off," the planner suggested.

"We probably will," Val said.

"I can't wait," the woman enthused. "I can't tell you how many brides want something other than a big tent. This sounds perfect."

"Be sure to read the literature in your goodie bag. And let us know if you need more information or a site tour."

After the women left, Russ looked at her. "You did that on purpose."

"They saw you hiding out over here and asked who you were. They thought you were a new wedding planner." Val grinned at his look of disbelief. "They perked right up when they heard you were an architect. I knew they wanted to meet you. Are you staying for Daddy's party?"

Russ considered the gift he'd picked up for Jacob Truelove last night. He'd enjoyed finding something the man would like. "If you're sure it's okay."

"Daddy likes you, Russ."

"I like him, too. And I'd love to stay if you think it won't be a problem."

"By now you surely know the Truelove motto."

"The more the merrier," Russ said, laughing with Val as they spoke the words together.

Later that afternoon they cleared the area in preparation for Saturday's wedding. Maddy had said they would be out on Friday to set up the tent for the reception. Russ stayed to help Val finish up after she sent Jane to the house to pick up Sammy. Afterward they walked up to the house together.

"Val, tell your father he has to go to the hospital," her mother said the moment they entered the living room.

She glanced from one to the other, wondering what was going on. Her dad sat in his recliner with his leg propped up, an ice bag against his head.

"Tell her," her mother insisted.

Her dad rolled his eyes. "Your mother is upset because Fancy nearly broke my leg today."

"And his head. You were unconscious, Jacob."

Val gasped and demanded, "Are you okay?"

"He doesn't know," her mother said, her voice rising almost hysterically. "He refuses to get himself checked out."

"Woman, it's my birthday," he growled. "My daughter has cooked all my favorite foods, and my family and friends will be here soon. I don't plan to sit around the emergency room and miss my own celebration."

"We could wait until you get back," Val suggested.

"Or we can celebrate now, and I could go to the hospital later if necessary. I wish I knew why Fancy went crazy like that."

"Is she okay?"

He shrugged. "Bill says she's calmed down. He put her in the stall and called the vet. We'll know more after Doc checks her out."

Cy rushed into the room and to his dad's side. "Mr. Bill said you were knocked unconscious."

"Bill has a big mouth," her father muttered.

"He was," her mother told their son.

"It takes more than a thump against the fence to break this hard head, Cindy."

"Let's hope so. One of these children should become a doctor."

"I plan to be a veterinarian," Cy volunteered.

"That should work for your father," she said with a stern look at her husband.

Val's father roared with laughter. "Woman,

I love you even when you nag me unmercifully."

She squeezed his hand, her eyes conveying that same love to her husband.

After a dinner of his favorites, her dad sat in his recliner with his leg propped up as he held court. Sammy had abandoned their mom in his favor. Val suspected it had to do with the presents that surrounded him. Little Sammy had all the Truelove men wrapped around her tiny fingers. All she had to do was flash that baby smile at them and they'd do anything for her.

"She's worried about his owie," her mom said as they watched them together.

"I know Dad loves that. Did she kiss him to make it better?"

Sammy was an energetic child, and they frequently had opportunities to kiss her owies away.

"At least twice on the cheek."

"Then I'm sure he's much better," Val assured her. "I'm so thankful he didn't get hurt worse."

"I still think he should be checked out."

"Maybe later," Val suggested.

"You know your dad. He'll pretend he's fine."

Val hugged her mom and sent up a quick prayer. "We're all keeping watch. Let him enjoy himself."

"I'm trying," her mother said before going over to sit in a chair next to her husband.

While the others visited, Val slipped out to the horse barn to check on Fancy. She pushed the metal stall door open, and when the horse pushed her head out the opening Val paused briefly to be certain Fancy had calmed down.

When the horse had first come to Sheridan Farm, her dad had expressed his belief that she was a winner. Because of his faith in her, Mr. Sheridan had named her Jacob's Fancy, and upon his death he'd left the horse to her father with permission to stable her on the farm for as long as he remained there.

Over the years their dad had taught them to exercise a great deal of care around the horses, and tonight more than ever before that training came to mind as Val assessed Fancy's current state. After determining the horse had returned to normal, she found a peppermint and held out her hand, palm up. Fancy took it and crunched the candy in her powerful teeth while Val rubbed the horse's forehead. "What happened today, girl?" she whispered. "Why did you act like that?"

"Everything okay?" Russ asked when he

located her in the horse barn.

Fancy's nicker of response gave her no answer.

"I hope so. She's in a delicate condition." She didn't share that the expected foal would be the result of a deal between his brother and her father. "What happened, Russ? Fancy has never acted like that before. Daddy could have been killed."

Russ slid his arm about her shoulder. "He's okay, Val. I don't imagine it's the first time he's been injured."

"No," she admitted, petting the horse when she butted her head against Val's shoulder, demanding attention. "He asked the vet to run tests."

"Good idea."

"I'm glad you stayed for the party. Daddy's enjoying himself."

"It's been fun. I was surprised to see Wendell."

"Opie invited him. I should have warned you he'd be here. Did you talk?" she asked almost hopefully.

"We exchanged pleasantries. I would have come anyway. I like your dad."

"He likes you."

"What about his daughter?"

"You're a great friend, Russ."

He looked disappointed. "Why do you

always qualify our relationship as friends?"

"Aren't we friends?" Val said.

"I think you know by now the pavilion is only an excuse to get out here and see you."

Val had seen the signs pointing in that direction and avoided the discussion until now. Sadness filled her as she considered how he would react to what she had to say. "We need to talk."

"Want to show me that Celtic knot garden in the moonlight?"

"Please, Russ, this is serious." Val knew Russ didn't have a clue as to what she needed to tell him. "Let's go to the Japanese garden," she said, hoping the beautiful area would provide the peace she was far from feeling. "I need to check to see that everything is in order for tomorrow."

Not sure where to start, she said, "When you consider the woman you will marry, I'm sure things you share in common are high on the list."

He took her hand, playing with her fingers for a moment before wrapping her hand securely in his. "It helps, but it's not a total necessity."

"Some things are important," Val said. "Couples have to be tolerant of their differences, willing to give and take, but there's one thing I'd never give on."

"What?" he prompted when she paused.

"My faith."

"I wouldn't expect that of you."

"But you could affect it in ways you can't begin to imagine. I could try to play God and hope I'd change your mind over time, but we know that doesn't happen. People don't change because that's what other people want. Marriage —"

"Whoa," Russ said. "Who said anything about marriage?"

"I did. For me the next logical step beyond friendship is love and marriage. I can like you as a friend or love you as a husband. There's no in-between ground."

"What happened to dating?"

"When I date I do so with marriage in mind," Val told him. "The man has to be as committed to me as I am to him. We'll come to know each other and our families well. We will have common goals and hopes for the future. Most important we will share a very spiritual relationship with our heavenly Father."

"And you don't see me as that man?"

"I'm sorry, Russ. If I allow our relationship to progress, we'll both end up getting hurt."

"No problem." He dropped her hand and left the bench, moving over into the shadowy edge of the garden.

She knew that wasn't true from the way his voice roughened. "Why are you angry?"

"I didn't think you were the manipulative type."

"I'm not."

"You're basically saying that unless I choose to follow your God you want nothing more to do with me."

"I never said that," Val cried out. "You're my friend. I'll always treat you as a friend."

"So I'm good enough to be a friend but no more in your life?"

"What do you expect, Russ? God comes first. He always has and always will. Every member of my family believes just as I do."

"Then you should warn your sister to steer clear of Wendell. He has less use for religion than I do."

"That's sad," Val said softly. "Jesus loves you. Why can't you love Him in return?"

Her question went unanswered. "I think I'll call it a night. Thank your parents for me."

"Russ?"

"Don't let it worry you, Val. It wouldn't work anyway. We want different things."

Later that night when Rom returned to the apartment, Russ sat on the sofa watching a sports program. "How's your dad?" he asked when Rom settled into the leather armchair.

Rom had remained at the house for a while to determine if his father needed to go to the emergency room. "Still insisting he's okay. I don't think they'll get him to the doctor. It was a great party. Opie outdid herself. That girl can cook."

"She can, and it was," Russ agreed, adding, "at least until the end."

"Why? What happened?" Rom asked.

"Your sister."

Rom leaned back. "What did Val do now?"

"Gave me the old we-can-be-friends spiel."

"You are friends. What's the problem?"

"I don't like being manipulated by women," Russ said. "I asked about dating, and she goes straight to marriage and how important it is that I share her faith."

"It's called being equally yoked."

Russ frowned. "You mean like a horse and wagon?"

"Actually that's a good simile. Think about what would happen if you stuck a racehorse in front of a freight wagon."

"It would be a bumpy ride."

"Exactly. Our parents taught us the importance of sharing relationships with believers. Friendship is nice, but love is better, and knowing that person is going to be around for the long haul makes all the difference."

"That's not always the case," Russ said. "Christians divorce."

"They do," Rom agreed. "Generally because they don't make God the head of their marriage."

"Why is God so important?" Russ muted the television and stuck a pillow under his head as he stretched out on the sofa. The brown leather squeaked with his movement.

"God is so much bigger than we can imagine. Haven't you ever wondered?"

"Not really. I attended church because it was mandatory. Not because I wanted to be there."

"Val's trying to tell you how she feels."

"That I'm not good enough for her because I don't love her God?" Russ demanded.

"Or you're good enough that she cares that you don't know God," Rom suggested. "She's only trying to keep you both from getting hurt in the long run."

"By rejecting me?"

"By being realistic. Val is not a manipulator. She's a good person who honestly cares about others. A rare jewel in today's world."

Russ knew Rom was right. Still, it pricked at him that she wouldn't consider furthering their relationship because of his lack of religion. "So what do you suggest I do?"

"Don't look at Val as a challenge because she says no," Rom said. "I like you, Russ, but don't fool around with my sister's heart."

Friend or not, Russ had no doubt the Truelove men would come after him if he tried. "She invited me to church a while back. Said an intelligent man ought to give God a chance before deciding not to follow him."

"Sounds like good advice to me," Rom agreed. "But it's doing what your heart leads you to do. Inviting people to church is like leading a horse to water. You can't make them drink living water either."

"Living water? What's that?"

"Jesus Christ is living water. Eternal life. In John 4:10 he spoke to the woman at the well and said, 'If thou knewest the gift of God, and who it is that saith to thee, Give me to drink; thou wouldest have asked of him, and he would have given thee living water.' "

Russ looked puzzled. "Why do you love God so much?"

"The relationship between God and man

is special. As corny as it may sound, I love Him because He first loved me. I try to act responsibly, but I sin. I'm human, and God knew I would. That's why He sent His Son to die on the cross for me. When I repent He forgives me, and I strive to do better."

"You do a lot of praying, too?"

"And Bible study. I plan to be active in my church, and those studies will help me with whatever role I'm asked to perform."

"You work in church, too?"

"Definitely. Faith without works is dead."

"Do you date?"

Rom smiled. "There's a woman who figures prominently in my future. She joined the Peace Corps after we graduated from UK. I plan to ask her to marry me when she comes home."

"Why didn't you go with her?"

"Not in the plans. I had a mission here at home. Before Val won the money, my role was to help provide for the kids who will soon graduate."

"What keeps you here now that Val set aside funds for their education?"

"I need to be here to support Val and my family. And I'm working toward my future with Stephanie. I can get started in my career and save for our future. Meanwhile, I plan to support Stephanie's work in Africa.

I want to visit her and make her life easier while she's there."

"You know, Rom, you Trueloves are too good to be true," Russ said.

"Mom always says the cream rises to the top."

He slung a sofa pillow in his friend's direction.

Rom caught it and laughed. "Don't get me wrong, Russ. We make mistakes and do stupid things, but we're a family with God at our center. And that does make a difference."

TWELVE

Their lives continued to change over the next weeks. One noticeable difference was the lack of Russ's presence in her life. Val knew he checked the job site and saw other members of her family but did everything possible to avoid her. Even when they talked on the phone he kept the conversation all business.

She missed him, but she knew the reason for the absence. Val still believed she'd made the right decision. She prayed, giving the situation over to God. Only He could open Russ's eyes to the fact that she cared enough for him to want his salvation.

Rom had shared some of his conversation with Russ and agreed Val had done the right thing. Russ's comment about Wendell had forced her to talk with Opie only to learn she and her sister were in the same situation. Both agreed the struggle to do right was even more difficult when the heart was involved.

The move to the Sheridan mansion was complete. They had all been teary-eyed when they closed the door on the empty house they had called home for so many years. Val had no doubt it would have been much worse if they had been required to leave the farm.

Living in a new place would be different, but from the first time she'd walked through the front door, Val had felt at home. Once the family agreed to make the move, she wanted them to feel the same way. She struggled to convince her parents to take the Sheridans' suite until they finally agreed. She, Opie, and Jules shared a guest wing and for the first time in their lives had rooms of their own with private baths. Roc and Cy opted to room together.

Heath would have his own room, but Rom would bunk with him during his frequent visits home.

But for now Heath slept in a downstairs bedroom. During the move he had tripped over Sammy on the stairs and sported a cast on his leg while the two-year-old wore one on her arm. Thankful their injuries hadn't been worse, Val insisted Heath follow the doctor's instructions. She missed him in their daily activities but knew he would have difficulty getting around on crutches.

Jane blamed herself, saying she should have taken Sammy home when Mrs. Cindy couldn't babysit. They had all reassured her, but she refused to be comforted. The situation worsened with the arrival of Jane's in-laws and Clarice Holt's demands to spend time with Sammy back at their hotel. When the child wanted nothing to do with the woman, Cindy Truelove suggested that the Holts along with Sammy and Jane stay in a couple of the guest rooms at the house so Sammy would be more comfortable. Clarice had gone out of her way to make everyone miserable, and the entire family had been happy to see her depart.

Despite her unhappiness, Val threw herself into making Your Wedding Place a success. Even though she had more than enough funds, she forced herself to be cautious with her expenditures. Your Wedding Place would operate in the black much sooner if she built the business slowly. Advertising drew a number of brides. Their frequent indrawn breaths of amazement assured her their efforts had been successful.

They hosted three receptions in September, and when the calls for corporate parties, bridal showers, engagement parties, and birthday events increased, they decided to try a few events. Despite their limitations, they had booked events into October.

Nearly a week of heavy rains had thrown the project schedule off even more. The sun had broken through over the weekend, and the construction crews had returned to work on Monday. The excavation work was nearly completed, and Todd Bigelow said they would be pouring concrete soon.

The gorgeous late summer days made her anxious to offer the pavilion as a venue. Several brides had booked for the coming year based on the drawings alone. Though some planned church weddings, they chose the pavilion for their reception site.

The need to talk to her dad had grown stronger with the passing of time, and Val awakened that morning with a plan to seek him out. She started across the yard and stopped to speak to Bill as he led a stallion across the yard. "He's a real beauty," she said, admiring the handsome animal from a distance.

Bill nodded. "I told Jacob he should think about buying him."

"Maybe he will," Val said before continuing her mission to find her dad. The scent of horses and leather filled her nostrils as she stepped into the farm office room. Opening his office door, she asked, "Got a minute?"

"Sure."

Val walked around the old metal desk and propped herself against the edge. "I don't want to upset you." That comment gained his attention. "But this has weighed on my heart for some time now. Daddy, will you go with me to visit Grandfather Truelove?"

His immediate withdrawal spoke volumes. "Why? What purpose would it serve?"

"I don't know," she answered honestly. "But I've prayed over the situation, and the only answer I can give you is it's time. When Jesus commissioned us to witness, don't you think He knew our family and friends would come first? How can we witness to Grandfather if we never visit him?" He remained silent. "I think maybe it's time I have an adult relationship with my grandfather."

Her dad pushed his chair back from the desk and stood. He walked over to the window and looked out. "He's been in prison longer than you've been alive. I tried to be a good son. When you and the twins were little, I took you to see him, thinking he might want to make a good impression on his grandchildren. He hardly spoke to you children. He only wanted to hear about the horses I worked with here at the farm. Wanted me to place a bet for him.

"Every visit was pretty much the same. The last time I went, he asked why Mom never contacted him. I told him we'd nearly lost her to a heart attack, and all he said was too bad. After that, I refused to go back. Those collect calls are the only contact we've had for years."

"Doesn't Grammy talk to him?"

"No. They're divorced. His creditors came after her when they couldn't get to him. She lived on disability, and we encouraged her to make their separation legal. She had done everything humanly possible to be a good wife and didn't need the added stress."

Val nodded. "How would you feel if he weren't your father?"

"I suppose I could summon more sympathy for a complete stranger dealing with the same demons."

"You've given up hope, haven't you?"

"Yes. I can't reach him."

"We'll respect your wishes," Val told her father, "but I think it's time we visited him. If you'd rather not go, I'll ask the others."

"Do you need an answer now?"

"No. I'm only asking that you pray over the situation."

Later that afternoon Val was working in the office when the doorbell rang. She was surprised when Russ walked into the room. Val thought he looked good in his worn jeans, golf shirt, and work boots. "What brings you out this way?"

"I needed to check the progress of the concrete pour and thought I'd say hello first. How's Heath?"

Val had wondered what made today's visit different. It hurt that he could remain friends with her family and not her. "Jane took him in for his doctor's appointment. He's hoping to get the cast off soon."

"Tell him I asked after him," he said. "I'd better get to the site."

Val refused to allow him to ignore her. "Mind if I ride out with you?"

As they walked out to the golf cart, Russ commented, "Looks like you've settled into the house well."

"It's been a process. We wanted to get moved before the kids went back to school."

"Where did the summer go?" Russ asked with a shake of his head.

"It's been a fast one. Jules is a senior this year."

"Still thinking about becoming an architect?"

"It's all she talks about. Thanks for inviting her to your office. You inspired her more than you know."

"At least I inspire one Truelove woman."

Val parked the cart at the job site. "Can't we get beyond this, Russ?"

Ignoring her question, he jumped out of the vehicle and walked over to look at the concrete pour for the lower structure walls that had occurred that day. He glanced back. "This isn't right."

"What do you mean?"

He pointed out the areas that were off. "What's going on here?" Russ demanded when Todd Bigelow joined them. "That concrete isn't poured according to the plans."

"You should know," the man said with a disapproving frown. "You sent that e-mail this morning an hour before the pour. We had a time making this many changes before the trucks came."

"I haven't sent any e-mails," Russ said, glancing at Val. "I met with a client all morning."

Todd pulled out his phone and pulled up the message. "Says it's from you."

"I didn't send that e-mail," Russ repeated. "I haven't done anything since you called yesterday and left a message that the pour was scheduled for today."

Seeing Russ's shocked expression, Val took the phone and studied the screen closely.

"It has your e-mail address."

"I can see that," Russ said, his voice rising with his frustration as he looked over her shoulder. "But I didn't send it."

"It's not my mistake. I shouldn't be expected to absorb the cost," Todd declared.

Val looked at Russ, and when he didn't speak she said, "Fix the problem. Mr. Hunter and I will work out the specifics."

"And don't act on any more e-mails until we get to the bottom of this," Russ warned.

"That's going to throw the schedule off even further," Val said after the man walked away, mumbling about modern technology.

"I didn't send it, Val."

She wanted to believe him, but all the evidence pointed directly to Russ. "Who else has access?"

"No one. I need a copy of that e-mail."

"What are we going to do about the cost?"

"I don't know that either," Russ said. "Mr. King will be upset when he learns about this mistake. It'll be costly to correct."

Anger shot through Val when Russ showed concern for his boss instead of her project. "And it's fair that I bear the cost?"

He cradled his head in his hands, burying his fingers in his hair. "I'm trying to figure this out. Don't do anything yet. Let me see if I can restructure the plans."

"And wait to have everything re-permitted? It would be quicker to break up the concrete and start over. I'll cover the costs, but I expect you to find out what happened."

"I want to know who did this, too."

Val called out to Todd. "Can you forward a copy of that e-mail to me? We need to look into this further."

"Yes, ma'am. There's something else. I got a call from the ironwork company demanding to know why we cancelled the order. They weren't happy when I told them I didn't know anything about a cancellation."

She looked at Russ again.

He looked stunned. "I haven't cancelled anything. That trim was special order. We need it on-site ready for installation."

"Something else you need to check into?" she asked with a frown.

Russ rubbed his face wearily. "Can we discuss this privately?"

At the house Val pulled up the e-mail and printed off a copy.

He read it again, the paper wrinkling with the pressure of his closed fist. "Todd left a message at the office yesterday saying the pour was today. That's why I came out this afternoon."

"You can send e-mail from anywhere with

your PDA."

He looked disappointed by her conclusion.

"But I didn't. I was in a meeting and didn't take it with me because the client hates interruptions and I didn't want to risk upsetting him."

"Well, somebody did, and I want to know who."

"So do I. You know I've been behind you and this project ever since I started the plans."

He relented at her look of disbelief. "Okay. Once I understood how important it was to you. And even if I didn't agree with you personally, I would not disrupt your project. My reputation is on the line."

"Well, someone did. How do you suggest we handle this?"

"I have a friend who knows computers. I'll see if he can help. I wouldn't do this, Val. I care too much for you to hurt you like that. I know what you said," Russ told her. "I can't turn my feelings on and off at will. I'm not trying to charm my way out of this mess. I'm being honest. I don't know who sent that e-mail or made the call, but I intend to find out."

"We should call Randall King."

"I'd like to talk with Jason first. See if he

can help me get a lead on where the e-mail originated."

Val tilted her head and looked at him curiously. "What aren't you telling me, Russ?"

"I'm asking you to trust me, but I can't say I'd blame you if you didn't."

"I might if you give me reason."

Russ sighed. "I don't know, Val. I don't want to go off halfcocked and make accusations that will destroy my career."

"What do you know?"

"Promise you'll keep this between us until we know for sure?" When she nodded, he said, "I overheard a phone conversation that I think had to do with you and Sheridan Farm. I think Randall King is part of this KFD Corporation that wants your farm."

"Is he behind the delays?"

"If he is he's covered his tracks well," Russ said.

"You don't trust him?"

"I never had a problem before."

"What's making a difference this time?" she asked curiously.

"You. I won't let him hurt you or your family."

She had her reason. "Okay, Russ, I'll give you a couple of days."

Back at the office, Russ contacted his friend

immediately. They had met in boarding school, and Jason had subsequently gone into the military and worked for the FBI.

"You've got to help me out, buddy," Russ said. "She thinks I did this."

"You have no idea who did?"

"No. I was in a meeting when it was sent. It's my e-mail address."

"Who has your password?"

"It's on file in the office. Randall King insists on that."

"Do you think King sent the e-mail?"

"Doesn't make sense he'd do something that would result in a major liability to his firm."

"Anybody there have a grievance against you?"

"Not that I'm aware of."

"It does seem more directed toward the Truelove woman," Jason commented. "She got problems with anyone in your office?"

"She's only worked with me."

"Can you have her send me the e-mail?"

"I have a copy I can fax right now."

"Do that but send me the real thing. Some people can hide their trail, but others don't realize it's there."

"Thanks, Jace. My integrity is at stake here."

"That something new you've picked up

since we used to hang out together?" his old friend joked.

"Yeah, since I grew up and got involved in the real world. This is important. I care what this woman thinks of me."

"It always involves a woman."

"The woman," Russ told him. "She's important to me, and we've already got enough issues. I don't want total lack of trust to become another."

"I'll get back to you as soon as I know something."

THIRTEEN

Every passing hour increased Russ's angst. He wanted to prove his innocence but didn't know how. He made several trips out to the site. He was thankful they had poured only a portion of the concrete. When he heard about the tear-out, Heath suggested using the concrete they removed for their landscaping projects. The new pour had taken place the day before, and the construction was back on track.

When he finally heard back from Jason, he took the evidence straight to Randall King. He was still reeling after learning the e-mail had come from their office using his e-mail address.

"Does Mr. King have any time open this morning?" Russ asked Cheryl.

She pulled up Mr. King's calendar on her computer. "He's free now."

"Please ask if he can see me."

While Russ worried about Randall King's

reaction, he also knew he had to do this for Val. No matter what the cost to his career, he owed her that much.

His boss looked up from his seat behind the massive desk when Russ entered. "What can I do for you this fine morning?"

"There's a problem with the Truelove project."

"With that contractor she chose," Randall said confidently.

"No, sir. Val made an excellent choice. I'm impressed by Todd Bigelow."

When there was no invitation to sit, Russ slid his hand into his pocket and fought the urge to jiggle coins.

"Then what's the problem?" Randall demanded, his gaze narrowing.

Russ slid the folder containing the information he'd gathered onto the desktop. "Someone sent this to her contractor using my e-mail."

"How is that possible?"

"I wondered the same thing. I was meeting with Harry Marshburn at the time. There's a statement in there attesting to the fact that I didn't send any e-mails while I was in his office.

"In fact I left my PDA in the car. Mr. Marshburn has a very strong dislike of interruptions, and I didn't want to take any chances. There's also a copy of the report where I logged the hours."

"And you have no idea where it was sent from?"

"I had my friend help determine the source, and it appears to have been generated from this office using my e-mail account."

"Are you accusing someone here of doing this?" Randall demanded.

"I'm telling you I was out of the office when it was sent and had no means of sending an e-mail so it had to be someone else. Val expects someone to cover her loss. A substantial loss. They had poured the concrete by the time I arrived that afternoon."

"This wouldn't have happened if she'd used Kevin."

"We don't know that to be the case. As I said, Todd Bigelow is proving to be a very competent contractor. I could see him handling future projects."

Randall flashed him a strange look. "How do you think we should proceed with this?"

"It's my understanding e-mail is forever."

"Who told you this?"

"My friend Jason. He's a computer expert with the FBI." Russ thought his boss looked surprised. "He says we can have the document retrieved. Meanwhile, I plan to change my passwords, and I won't be sharing them with anyone. I've also directed Todd not to make any future changes unless he hears them directly from my lips."

"Has Ms. Truelove spoken about suing the firm?"

"She's very upset," Russ confirmed. "I wouldn't be surprised if she's consulted her attorney regarding the matter."

"Can the floor plan be reworked to accommodate the error?"

"I suggested that, but Val was more concerned about the time involved in re-permitting. She ordered it ripped out. I understand her concern. We've already had another delay with a document missing from the initial plan submission."

"Why wasn't I informed about that?"

"She called me after her contractor checked online and saw the plans had been rejected. I was able to resolve the matter and get the permit issued without further delay."

"I don't care for my firm looking bad to the clients."

"I don't care for being made to look bad either," Russ said. "I didn't send that e-mail, and until we figure out who did we have a problem."

"I'll handle it."

"There's something else," Russ said. "A woman called the ironworks company and cancelled the order. She used Val's name. Luckily they contacted Todd, and we got the job order reinstated. I don't know what's going on, but I don't like it one bit. What do I tell Val Truelove?"

"That I'm looking into the situation," Randall King said brusquely.

Back in his office, Russ called to tell Val exactly what his boss had said to tell her. The desire to share Jason's information was strong, but company loyalty forced him to keep silent. Still, that didn't mean he wouldn't continue investigating things on his own. Someone was after Val, and he wanted to know why.

Fourteen

When Russ told her his boss was looking into the situation, Val recognized the message for what it was — a delay tactic. Still, she'd witnessed Russ's shock and believed he intended to protect them. That's why she'd promised to trust him — why she'd prayed he could prove his innocence.

A more important family matter took precedence in the Truelove household. Her father had agreed to visit Mathias Truelove, and Val didn't plan to give him time to change his mind. After much discussion, Val, Opie, Rom, and Heath decided to go with him to visit their grandfather Truelove at Kentucky State Penitentiary. Her father insisted Jules, Roc, and Cy stay at home with their mother. Val respected his need to protect the younger children.

They left after lunch to drive up to Eddyville and spend the night in a hotel to be there for the 7:30 a.m. visiting hour the following day.

As they approached the prison, Val remembered the imposing structure from her childhood. "I can see why they call it the castle," she told the others.

"Has a definite European flair," Opie agreed.

"Are you sure you want to do this?" their father asked. "We can still turn back."

"We need to do this, Daddy."

Resigned to his fate, Jacob Truelove nodded. A few minutes later they entered the room where the older version of their father waited. Prison had aged him far beyond his sixty-seven years, and the standard issue clothing seemed a bit loose on his sparse frame. His back stooped slightly when he stood.

"I was surprised when your dad said you were coming to visit. You're all grown up." He glanced at his son. "So, Jake, tell me who's who."

"This is my eldest, Valentine," he said, laying his hand on first Val and then Opie's shoulders. "Our second daughter, Ophelia. And our twins, Romeo and Heathcliff."

"Never did understand why you let that woman of yours hang those names on your kids."

"Our children," Val's father told him.

"Cindy had as much of a right to choose their names as I did."

"Still cranky as ever, aren't you, boy?"

As the two of them glared at each other, Val realized how alike and yet how different they were. Their appearance might be similar, but their personalities were worlds apart. "Please don't argue."

Her grandfather looked at her, started to say something, and stopped. "So what have you children been doing?"

"Rom and I just completed our MBAs at Harvard, sir," Heath said.

The old man looked unimpressed. "What happened to your leg?"

Though he no longer used crutches, Heath wore a brace.

"Fell down the stairs."

"Too bad."

Val glanced at her father, aware he remembered a time his father had used those same words many years before.

"And I graduated from culinary school," Opie said, picking up where Heath left off.

"A cook, huh? We could use a good one around this place."

"Actually a chef," Opie told him.

"Ain't that a fancy name for a cook?" he demanded, not waiting for an answer. "And you, Valentine — Jake tells me you had a bit

225

of luck with the lottery."

"I didn't tell you anything," her father said.

"Please, Daddy," Val said.

Her grandfather shrugged. "Must have heard it somewhere else. You take after your old grandfather and enjoy playing games of chance?"

Val shook her head. "No, sir. Daddy doesn't allow us to gamble." He looked confused. "I prayed, and God provided."

The older man looked at his son. "You filled their heads with that nonsense?"

"Believing in God isn't nonsense," Heath told him. "In fact, it's pretty smart."

"God never did anything for me."

"You never did anything for Him either," their father said.

"Save your talk, boy. I already have enough people preaching to me."

"We won't apologize for loving the Lord," Val told him.

"So how did you win the lottery?"

"The ticket was a gift from my boss."

The old man laughed and slapped his hand against his leg. "Talk about luck. Wouldn't be here today if I'd had a bit of that myself."

"We consider it a blessing," their father told him.

Ignoring his son's words, he asked Val, "What are you doing with your money?"

"Investing in our future and helping others by meeting their needs. We've donated food and clothing to the homeless shelter, supported mission work in Africa, funded scholarships, and paid for church camp for needy kids. We've helped families with financial problems caused by major illness and were blessed to be able to help another family who lost their home to fire —"

"Doesn't sound like fun to me," he interrupted.

Her father grunted, and Val squeezed his arm in a gesture of comfort. "We never needed money to enjoy ourselves," she assured her grandfather.

"You still run that farm?" Mathias Truelove asked his son.

"Yeah," he answered, his tone surly and unfriendly.

"What are you kids gonna do with your lives?"

All throughout the trip their father had cautioned them not to share their private business with their grandfather. He'd even made them promise not to trust too quickly. "I'm working with a wedding venue business," Val said.

"Landscape work," Heath said when his

grandfather looked at him.

"Not much of a job with that fancy education of yours."

"It's good for now," Heath said.

"And you?" he said, looking at Rom.

"I took a consulting job."

His grandfather nodded approval. "And what about you, missy?" he asked, directing his question at Opie.

"I'm helping out around home, but I've done some catering and worked as a personal chef."

"Goofing off, huh?"

"She just got out of school," Val said.

Her grandfather looked at her. "Lots of restaurants out there. Shouldn't take long to find work if she's good."

"I'm very good," Opie said.

He allowed his gaze to move from face to face. "I have some good-looking grandkids. Ain't there more of your kids?"

"Jules, Roc, and Cy are at home with Mom," Val said.

"Why didn't they come?"

"I didn't feel it was a good idea," her father told him.

"Did you bring pictures?" he asked. When his son shook his head, the older man asked, "How's Lena doing?"

Her father's voice tightened as he spoke

about his mother. "She has her ups and downs. Karen called last week and said they're running more tests."

"Takes after her mother with that heart disease," their grandfather said with a shake of his head. "She's a good woman. Too good for the likes of me. It's great seeing all of you. I don't usually have visitors."

The thought saddened Val. For thirty years her grandfather had sat in prison, alone, believing no one cared anything about him. Wasn't that punishment enough for his mistakes?

He asked questions and rambled on until they ended visiting hours. "It's been mighty fine seeing all of you today. I hope you'll come back and bring the other kids."

"That was really heartbreaking," Val said as they climbed into the SUV for the drive home.

"He doesn't deserve better."

"Do you really believe that, Daddy?"

"Yes, Val. I have asked God to help me forgive him, but I can't. Every time they put Mom into the hospital I get angry all over again."

"But you heard what he said. Grammy's mom had heart problems, too. You've never sent him pictures of us?"

"No. And I don't plan to start now."

"What harm would it do?"

"Think about it, Val. He's in prison for life, knows you have money, and knows people who would do anything to get a bit of that money."

His succinct answer hit home. Mathias Truelove had failed his son in every way possible. "Uncle Zeb and Aunt Karen don't visit either, do they?"

"He got to you, didn't he?"

"I feel for him. He sits in prison day in and day out with no family who loves him, and he makes the occasional collect call to children who couldn't care less if they hear from him. What encourages or motivates him to be a better man?"

"That's the point, Val," her dad said, his voice rough and unfeeling. "Nothing motivates him. You heard him today."

"I did. I do feel sad for him. In fact, I feel sad for every man in that prison."

"Well, I don't. Every one of them is getting exactly what he deserves."

"There but for the grace of God," Val said softly. "Would you love us any less if we had made wrong decisions and ended up there?"

"You know I wouldn't."

Silence stretched as they drove toward home. Val dealt with today's visit in the only way she knew how. Prayer. Only God could heal the rift between father and son.

Fifteen

The pavilion project was well underway by the time she received a call from Randall King asking her to come to his office. Val wondered why Russ hadn't contacted her but assumed Mr. King had taken control because of his firm's liability. She'd asked her lawyer to accompany her, and they waited in the Prestige Designs conference room.

Randall King and Russ entered together, and his boss chose the seat at the head of the table while Russ sat on the opposite side facing her. Randall King began with an apology. "I'm sorry this happened, and I assure you Prestige Designs will accept responsibility for the incident."

"I don't know how it happened, but there are questions I'd like answered," Russ said. The situation became even more tense when Russ confronted his boss with his concerns. "I overheard you telling someone

Val would probably lose interest soon enough and sell the property."

"I never said any such thing," Randall denied.

"You might not have called her by name, but it was very clear who you were talking about," Russ said. "And I've learned you're a partner in this KFD Corporation that made an offer for Sheridan Farm."

"What's your point, Russ?" he demanded. "Are you accusing me of sabotaging a client's project? If so, I hope you're prepared to prove that's the case."

"I'm not accusing you of anything," Russ said. "I'm stating facts. I overheard you talking about Val's business. You made an offer to buy the farm after Prestige had taken on the project."

"Yes, we wanted the land," Randall admitted. "It's an excellent location, and we had plans to build several multimillion-dollar homes. But when Sheridan sold it to the Trueloves, we realized that wouldn't happen."

"Then why make the offer? That's why you were so insistent I use Kevin Flint," Val guessed. "You knew he'd take his time and thought it would discourage me enough to sell, didn't you?"

"You hired your own contractor," Randall

said in answer to her accusation.

"You were angry Val rejected Flint," Russ said. "So much so that you kept insisting I wrap up her project and move on. We've never done that to another client."

"Look. I'm not the bad guy here," Randall told Val, ignoring Russ's comment. "I didn't do anything to affect your project. In fact, I had my IT staff continue what Russ started with the e-mail research and learned where it generated. That's why I brought you in today."

"I'm glad you didn't just let it drop," Val said.

"As I told Russ, I don't like looking bad to my clients. Now that I know who sent the e-mail, I accept full responsibility. I'll give you a check for your losses before you leave here today."

Val glanced at Russ. His left eyebrow shot up a fraction, and he shrugged when Mr. King asked Cheryl to join them in the conference room.

When the door opened, everyone's gaze focused on the new arrival. Val recognized the secretary and wondered what she had to do with the situation. Randall directed her to have a seat.

Val felt almost sorry for the woman as she scurried to a chair next to Russ. Her nervous demeanor was that of a person with something to hide. After seating herself, she carefully arranged her pad and pen on the tabletop and looked expectantly at her boss.

"Cheryl, we have an incident regarding an e-mail that was sent from this office using Russ's e-mail address. It's been traced back to your computer."

"Everyone uses my computer," she said, immediately going on the defensive. "I've asked them not to, but they won't listen."

"Russ has an alibi in this instance," Randall told her. "He has a client who recalls their meeting and stated he did not send any e-mails during the time they were together."

Cheryl glanced at the pad of paper. "Why would anyone use his e-mail address? We all have our own."

"Because this person obviously wanted to cause trouble," Randall told her. "In this case, the incident cost Ms. Truelove several thousand dollars which Prestige will have to absorb."

Cheryl's pale skin went even whiter.

Randall King didn't let up on his attack. "Russ requested help from the FBI, and it has been determined the e-mail was sent from your computer. Do you have something to share with us regarding the situation?"

Silence stretched in the room as no one spoke. Finally she looked up, tears trailing down her face. She swiped at them ineffectually and admitted, "I did it."

"Why?"

"Because Derrick asked me to."

"Derrick?" Randall King repeated.

"Derrick Masters?" Val demanded.

Cheryl sniffed back tears and nodded, her voice almost inaudible when she continued speaking. "I thought he loved me. He talked about getting married, and then he ran off with that woman he met at one of his weddings."

Everyone around the table shared looks but kept quiet as she continued.

"Derrick and I met when I came to work for Prestige two years ago. He saw me in the parking lot and came over to introduce himself. He asked me out, and we've dated ever since."

Val wondered if Cheryl knew about all the other women Derrick had dated.

"He worked hard for Maddy. We only saw each other for lunch some days and then the occasional weekend. He said he was doing it for us," she added, her voice changing with emotion.

Val felt sorry for the woman. Derrick had lied to her. His work schedule was nothing like he'd led her to believe.

The not-so-young woman looked at Val. "I know what I did was wrong, but I loved him."

"So you admit to sending the e-mail," Randall said, his face expressionless. "What else?"

"I called and cancelled the iron work order. Derrick said we had to pay her back. Said the money should have been his." Her accusatory gaze fixed on Val. "Derrick said Maddy started to hand him the lottery ticket, and then you walked up, and she handed it to you instead."

The depths of Derrick Masters's deception astonished Val. "That's ridiculous. He hadn't even come to work when Maddy arrived that morning."

Cheryl's mouth dropped open.

"Anything else?" Randall asked.

"I took information from the plans before I delivered them," she confessed. "I never believed he'd take advantage of me like this. He knew I'd do anything for him."

Val didn't doubt Derrick would take advantage of his mother if he had one. Feeling sorry for the misguided woman, she made a decision to forgive. "I won't file charges."

"Oh, thank you," Cheryl cried. "I can't speak for Mr. King," she warned.

Cheryl glanced at her boss and back at Val. "Derrick is a rat," she pronounced vehemently. "There was something else. He thought it was so funny. He left your launch party at Sheridan Farm early and managed to feed one of your horses drugged sugar cubes."

"Are you sure?" Val demanded.

Cheryl nodded. "I remember how happy he was to have rubbed his presence in your face. He tried to stir up the planners to ask questions about your money instead of your new venture. Said you didn't like talking about winning the lottery. When that didn't work he left early.

"He was furious that you'd done so well with your business. I wouldn't be surprised if he's picking the new wife's pockets to come up with funding to start a similar business. He thought it was the ultimate payback. Said you'd never figure out it was him."

"My father was injured because of that incident," Val told her. "The horse reacted very badly and threw him against a fence. He was knocked unconscious and hurt his leg on his birthday."

"Oh!" Cheryl cried, covering her mouth with her hand. "I'm so sorry."

"Derrick is fortunate Daddy didn't suffer any long-term consequences," Val said, anger rising up in her throat at the thought of anyone doing something so evil. "Though I'm not sure what decision my father will make regarding Derrick's actions when he learns the truth. That horse and the foal she's carrying are very important to him and worth a considerable sum."

"I hope he makes him pay," Cheryl said, emotion fueling her fury.

A few moments of silence and uncomfortable stirring followed her words.

"You can go back to your desk, Cheryl," Randall told her. "Don't leave the building. We're not finished with this discussion."

"Yes, sir."

Val looked at Russ. "I'm sorry. I shouldn't have doubted you."

"I understand," he told her, his eyes communicating his sincerity. "You couldn't know Derrick and Cheryl were involved. I didn't either. I suspected Mr. King, and I should have shared the truth with you sooner. I let cowardice stand in the way of protecting you."

"I didn't do anything," Randall objected.

"Only because God protected Val's family

from your efforts," Russ told him.

"None of these incidents had anything to do with me," Randall King declared.

"Why did Cheryl deliver the plans?" Val asked. "Russ told me you always do that."

"I was tied up and asked Cheryl to leave work early and take them."

"I knew that package was complete when I handed it over," Russ said.

"Here's your money," Randall said, pushing a company check across the table. "I can only apologize and assure you nothing like this will happen again."

Val pushed the check back. "I meant what I said. I'll absorb my loss. I won't file charges either." Rolling her chair back, she stood. "You have to make your decision, but she's more victim than criminal. Thank you for resolving this matter.

"I do have another request," she said, glancing over at Russ and then back at Randall King. "Russ is a good friend, and the stance he's taken today has been in my defense. I'm asking that you do the honorable thing and not seek retribution. He battled company loyalty against our friendship, but he's also been dedicated to his work here at Prestige. I haven't made it easy for him. I've put him in tough situations, but he's done a commendable job. He will make a fine architect, and I don't want his internship to suffer because of this incident."

"I'll take your request under advisement," Randall agreed.

Val tapped the check and reminded him, "Do unto others, Mr. King."

Respect filled the man's expression as he nodded.

The attorney paused to speak to Randall King, and Russ followed Val from the conference room. He waited while she walked over to the front desk and spoke to Cheryl. The gratitude on the woman's teary-eyed face spoke volumes.

"What did you say to her?" Russ asked.

"That I was sorry Derrick misled her. I can't believe he took advantage of her like that. I'm furious he caused that accident. Daddy could have been killed."

"Anyone know where he is?"

"No."

"The police would find him if you filed charges."

"I plan to tell Daddy and leave the decision to him."

"Good idea," Russ agreed. "Thanks for what you said in there."

"Thanks for doing what you did," Val said. "I know it was difficult to risk your standing in the firm."

"Not really," Russ admitted. "Lately I've learned doing the right thing might not be easy, but it makes you feel better about yourself."

Val wished she felt better. Blaming Russ had been easy. She called herself his friend, but she hadn't trusted him. "I'm so sorry I doubted you."

"I'm ready to put this behind us. I want to finish your project."

"I don't think anyone else could do it justice," she said.

Their gazes met and held. "Thanks. Can I come over tonight to talk? Just hear me out. That's all I'm asking."

She owed him that much. "You want to come for dinner?"

"Not tonight. I'll be there around eight if that's okay."

"I'll see you then."

Val barely touched her meal as she considered what Russ wanted to discuss. Anxiety filled her as she wondered if he thought they could pick up where they had left off. Val wished they could. Why couldn't things be different? She'd been so relieved today to learn he hadn't been involved.

When he arrived Russ spent a few minutes discussing their meeting with Val and her family before he asked if she'd like to visit the site with him. She drove the golf cart and parked near the structure.

"I know you wonder what's on my mind."

Val nodded.

"I care about you, and while I consider you a friend my feelings go much deeper."

"Why are you telling me this, Russ? Nothing has changed."

"It has. I have." His earnest declaration reached out to her in the darkness. "I need to understand what you expect from me."

Puzzled, Val said, "I can't expect anything of you. The decision is yours."

"What if I said I'd like to take you up on your offer to visit your church?"

"There's nothing I'd love more, but I'd ask why."

"That's fair," Russ said. "I really want to put this behind us, but you need to hear this. I haven't felt this alone since my parents died. I didn't know how to prove my innocence. I didn't even know what would happen when we walked into that conference room today. Once Randall King took over the investigation, he shut me out. I think he had his doubts about where my loyalties lay.

"But God has been busy in my life. Rom picked up where you left off. I couldn't understand why a loving God could let my parents die in that horrible accident or have Wendell betray me. Anger has controlled my life for years, and I haven't wanted to let go. One night we sat down to dinner, and Rom prayed that God would protect me from all harm.

"It threw me back to a time in school when I pulled another crazy stunt and the doctor said God must be working overtime to protect me. I wondered how that could be. God never had any reason to care about me. I found myself needing Him to care. I dug out my Bible and tried to go it alone, but I needed spiritual feeding. I went to church and enjoyed the experience."

Surprised by his revelation, Val asked, "What have you decided?"

"That I'm committed to developing a relationship with my Savior. I know I have a long road ahead of me. I'm taking baby steps. Trying to understand where I fit in." Russ smiled. "I took a wise woman's advice and did what she said a smart man would do. I'm finding my answers."

Joy blossomed within her like a glorious rose on a sunny day. "I can't tell you how happy that makes me."

"Because we're friends?"

"Yes," Val said. "Definitely that, but I

wanted you to know the peace that only God can give you."

"I want to know it."

She grinned. "Can I hug my dear friend?"

Russ opened his arms, and Val leaned forward, into the arms of the man she loved with all her heart.

SIXTEEN

"I'm sorry the pavilion isn't ready for the party," Russ said the morning of her mother's birthday. He had arrived with Rom the previous evening and stayed to help them set up for the events.

They planned a day of parties for her mother's celebration. The day event included family, friends, and the entire church. There were games and activities, and Opie had planned an extensive barbecue luncheon. That night they would celebrate with family and close friends with a dinner at the house.

"Just gives us a good reason to plan another reunion for the spring," Val assured him with a smile. "Aren't the gardens beautiful?"

Not as beautiful as the woman who stood before him, Russ thought. "We'd better get busy. The guests will be arriving soon."

He remained by her side as they completed the million-and-one tasks. Her mother was very surprised, and it was a wonderful day; but by that afternoon, Val was exhausted. She found her paternal grandmother inside the tent and hugged her. "It's so good to see you, Grammy."

"You should visit me more often."

Val dropped into the chair next to her. "The business keeps me occupied."

Her grandmother Truelove nodded. "Your dad keeps me updated on what you've been doing. I'm proud of the way you've handled this situation."

Val smiled her thanks. "You could come and spend time with us now. There's a guest room."

After her last heart attack, Lena Truelove hadn't been able to travel much. She lived in an assisted living apartment in Florida, and her daughter, Karen, who lived nearby, checked on her daily. "Has Jacob adapted to living in the big house yet?"

"He's trying."

The two women shared a familiar smile. "I'd love to see that for myself. Probably want to wait until it's warmer though. These old bones have adapted to Florida weather. And who is this young man I've seen you with today?" she asked, indicating Russ who stood nearby talking with her uncle Zeb.

Val motioned him over. "This is Russell Hunter. Russ, this is my grandmother, Lena Truelove."

"My pleasure, ma'am," he told her with a big smile.

"I've wanted to meet Val's young man ever since her daddy told me about him."

Val felt the blush warming her skin in the cool November air. "Oh, he's not . . . what did Daddy say?"

"He mentioned Russ about the time he started coming to the farm. Jacob says there's something about the two of you together. He had a feeling."

Val glanced at Russ and said, "We certainly argued enough in the beginning."

"But you like me now," Russ said confidently.

Her grandmother chuckled. "Your dad told me about visiting his father. Thank you for that."

While Val believed God had directed her in the situation, she could only hope she'd handled it in the right way. When she shared her concerns with Russ, he suggested she give it time. He'd reminded her the situation hadn't developed overnight.

"You think it was a good idea?"

Lena nodded. "Your dad has been angry with his father for a very long time. Jacob is a good man, but he's letting this stand in the way of his complete fulfillment with God. It's time he let it go."

"He was furious when Grandfather Truelove learned about the money."

Her grandmother's soft smile told Val she understood her son. "Jacob's afraid for you, honey. Mathias won't help himself. I knew he had problems when we met, but I allowed myself to hope."

"He asked about you," Val said.

Her grandmother's smile was bittersweet. "I loved him. In some ways I still do, but I'm a much wiser woman since I started thinking with my head instead of my heart."

Val glanced at Russ. She knew he'd read her mind.

"Jacob blamed his father for so much, but the decisions were mine. I could have said no."

"Why didn't you?" Russ asked.

"The others wised up to him pretty quickly, but I gave Mathias chance after chance. I hoped he'd prove everyone wrong."

"You loved him that much?"

"He was my husband. After I committed to your grandfather and the children came along, I did what I had to do to keep my family intact. He might not have been much of a husband or father, but he was all we had. I have my regrets. Between us we forced Jacob to grow up too fast. He was determined none of them would follow their father's example. No child should have to shoulder that kind of burden at such a young age."

"I don't know if we'll ever reach Grandfather Truelove, but I know we have to try."

"Keep at it, Val. You'll make a difference. And I might just go with you one of these days and see Mathias myself."

The comment surprised her. Val knew her grandmother's health had deteriorated after her grandfather's incarceration. The first heart attack had nearly killed her, but her children had rallied around to protect and care for her. More scary times had come up in the intervening years, but God had answered their prayers and kept her with them. "I doubt you could talk Daddy into that."

"You forget I'm his mother," she said, her brown eyes so much like those of her son and granddaughter. "If I say I want to go he won't like it, but he'll take me."

"Pray for him, Grammy."

"I do, honey. Every day of my life I pray for each one of you. Now you two run on

250

and spend time with your mother. It's her day."

Later that evening, after they had dressed for dinner, Val and Russ took a walk out to the pavilion. They stood atop the structure looking out into the distance. The beauty of fall surrounded them in the glorious russet reds, oranges, and golds of the trees and the glow of a beautiful sunset.

"Can you imagine how this will look come spring?"

"I'm told by a very reliable source it will be spectacular," Russ teased.

"Just wait and see," Val said.

"I plan to be right here. I've enjoyed hearing myself referred to as Val's young man today."

"I'm so embarrassed. My family gets carried away at times."

"I like that about them," Russ said. "It's good to be around people who say and do what they feel without hesitation."

"Oh, that's always a definite in this group."

Silence stretched for a couple of minutes as they both looked out over the vista.

Russ turned to face her and reached for her hand. "Val, I'm very glad to have you as my friend."

She squeezed his hand. "I learned a valuable lesson on friendship and trust from you."

"From me?"

She nodded. "You can't have one without the other. I said you were my friend; but when things got bad I didn't trust you, and that was wrong."

"But I understood why."

"Not at first. You were hurt and angry and wanted nothing to do with me, but you didn't let it stand in the way of looking out for me when things got bad."

"Because I care for you."

"I know. And I care for you."

"Enough to consider me as a potential future mate?"

The breath rushed from her chest. "Do you understand where this is headed if I say yes?"

"Just so you're clear on my intentions, I want to spend time getting to know you and your family better with the intention of holy matrimony in our future."

"What about your family? Did you see Wendell today?" Val asked, hopeful Russ had taken a step toward healing their relationship. He nodded, and she knew without asking that they hadn't spoken to each other. "At least talk to him, Russ. He's your brother."

"Why do you insist when you know how I feel?"

"Didn't you hear anything Grammy said today about forgiveness? Do you really want to waste years of your life hating your brother? Just listen to what he has to tell you."

Russ frowned and asked suspiciously, "What do you know, Val?"

"Wendell told Opie his mother left Hunter Farm to him."

"His mother?"

Val nodded. "It was part of her inheritance. The will stipulated that the farm go to her firstborn son."

"But it has Dad's name."

"I don't know the specifics, but I'm sure Wendell will tell you if you asked."

"Why hasn't he said something before now?"

"Would you have listened?"

"No," he admitted guiltily. "My determination to play judge and jury didn't provide much opportunity for him to share the truth."

"He's your brother, Russ. That didn't change because you were angry with him."

"I've shut him out for too long, Val. He's not going to talk to me."

"Your job is to seek forgiveness. His is to

253

forgive. If you're truly committed to changing your life, you have to do this."

"You never stop asking the impossible of me."

"It isn't as impossible as you believe. You can live out your days on earth without your family, or you can enrich your life and Wendell's by being his brother. One day you'll be an uncle to his children. Do you want to miss out on that because of something so silly?"

"Not if what you say is true."

"Opie got it straight from Wendell's lips."

Russ shook his head sadly. "Dad always made such a big deal about a man being the breadwinner for his family. Now I'm thinking maybe he said that to cover his shame because Wendell's mom provided his livelihood."

"I'm sure your father did his part to make the farm successful," Val said. "Neither you nor Wendell has ever lacked for anything."

"That's true."

"I don't want money or possessions to come between us."

"We won't let them."

"They came between you and Wendell."

"Because I was young and foolish and thought I knew everything," Russ said. "I've changed, and I promise you now that we'll take all the time we need to come to an agreement over our future. I know you have the money, and I will support you in the decision-making process."

"Finances could play a major role in our relationship."

"Not if we give control over to God. If we seek Him in our decision making, we will always make the right choice."

"We will," she said, smiling. "And, yes, I'd love to get to know you better with the intention of becoming your wife."

Russ hugged her, swinging Val about in his joy. Their laughter floated in the evening air.

"Sorry to interrupt, but Opie says it's time for dinner." They turned in the direction of her dad's voice as he walked toward them.

"Good. I'm starved," Val said.

"Russ, can I have a couple of minutes with my daughter?"

"Yes, sir. I'll tell everyone you're on the way."

After Russ disappeared down the stairs, Val asked, "What's wrong, Daddy?"

"I didn't mean to eavesdrop, but what you said to Russ about his brother . . . that applies to me and my father, too." His voice choked up, and tears spilled from his eyes. "For years I've blamed him for the things he did, certain he could have been different if he'd loved us enough. I call myself a Christian, but I forgot one major thing. Forgiveness. I need to forgive my father. I don't want to hate him anymore."

Val wrapped her arms about his waist. "Then forgive him, Daddy. Tell him and know you're a better person because you no longer harbor that anger. Pray that God will open his eyes to the life he's living and turn him around so we'll see him in heaven one day."

"I'm with Russ on this one. It seems impossible."

"Haven't you always told us nothing is impossible when God is in it? Pray for the right words and the strength to do what you need to do. I'll pray, too. And if you want, I'll be right by your side when you go to tell him."

"I love you, Valentine. You know, I never considered just how much parents learn from their children. You're one wise young lady."

"Who has been blessed with very wise parents," she told him. "Daddy, will you help me help Russ through this situation with Wendell? He needs to seek his brother's forgiveness, too."

"We'll all help each other. You made a very

strong point for Christianity today, Valentine. We both got the message loud and clear."

Russ nearly did a jig as he ran down the steps and toward the house. She'd agreed to consider a future with him. The utter hopelessness that had filled him for so long had lessened with his growing relationship with God. The hope Val had given him for their future and the love he had for her made him happier than he'd thought possible.

The last few weeks had definitely been a season of growth in his personal life. The pastor's sermon on that first Sunday he'd attended church had been on persecution. Russ identified with his subject. While Russ understood his experience was nothing like that of Jesus Christ, he couldn't help but wonder why things happened as they did. That morning's scripture had been Hebrews 13:6, "So that we may boldly say, The Lord is my helper, and I will not fear what man shall do unto me."

Russ remembered sitting in the pew after the sermon ended, his head filled with all he had heard and read. He reread the scripture. Was this how Val handled the situations that confronted her?

When Pastor Henry came to stand by the pew and asked if everything was okay, Russ glanced up. "Yes, sir. I was thinking about your sermon."

They discussed the message for a few minutes before the pastor asked, "What brought you to our church, Russ?"

The truth poured from him like water from a pitcher. "Something happened, and all fingers pointed to me. I'm innocent, and the one person I wanted to trust me most had doubts. I understood why . . ."

"But they hurt?"

"Yes, sir, they did."

"Why do you suppose that happened?"

"I acted in a way that led her to have those doubts."

"But if she's a friend . . ."

"She is. She worries about my salvation."

"Ah," Pastor Henry said with a nod of his head. "A very good friend indeed."

"I'm beginning to see that more clearly every day. When I asked her out she refused. I thought she had played me along, but then I realized she's standing up for her beliefs."

"Sounds like she's more than a friend."

"I'd like for her to be. That's one of the reasons I'm here." When Russ saw his words displeased the man, he said, "I know the most important reason is to get to know

Jesus as my Savior."

Pastor Henry nodded. "And have you?"

"I'm working on it. God was never part of my life so I didn't feel any connection. It's only since I met this wonderful family that has God at their center that I've begun to wonder."

"Are you open to the possibilities?"

"I think so. Her brother has helped me understand so much. He attends with me when he can, but he's very active in his own church."

"Why didn't you go there?"

"I didn't want to raise their hopes. If this doesn't work out . . ."

"Do you doubt it will?"

"No, sir. In fact, my mind is clearer than it's been in a very long time."

Pastor Henry smiled. "Would you care to join us for lunch?"

Russ stood quickly, gathering his papers together and stuffing them into his Bible. "I'm sorry. I'm holding you up."

The man patted his shoulder kindly. "They know not to wait on me. My wife has kept many a plate warm while I minister to my flock. Feel free to talk to me anytime you feel the need."

Russ thanked the pastor for his time and left. He'd taken the man up on his offer in

259

the passing weeks. Pastor Henry had helped him a great deal.

Too bad he wasn't around now to help him talk to Wendell. Russ dreaded the conversation. He'd misjudged Wendell, and now he had to make it right. No time like the present, he thought as he let himself into the house.

SEVENTEEN

"Will these do for where you're taking me tonight?" Val asked as she entered Opie's room carrying a pair of boots. She wore the long-sleeved, jewel-toned wool dress Opie said would look nice and help ward off the winter chill.

"They're fine," Opie said. "You might as well give up, birthday girl. It's a surprise, and you're not going to get it out of me. And would you please stop moping around like you've lost your best friend?"

Val looked meaningfully at the vase of roses sitting on Opie's nightstand. "At least the man in your life remembered Valentine's Day. You should have gone out with him. You would have had more fun."

Opie walked closer and rubbed two fingers together in Val's face. "Know what this is? The world's smallest violin player. The poor-little-me act isn't working."

Val laughed. "Okay. I'll try to have fun."

"That's all I'm asking." Opie walked away and paused at the window. "Looks like someone left the pavilion lights on again."

Dropping onto the side of the bed, Val tugged on her boots. "I'll run out and turn them off while you finish dressing."

"I'll be ready by the time you get back," Opie promised before she disappeared into the bathroom.

Val wondered where everyone was as she walked through the house, pausing in the mudroom to pull on her coat. In the garage, she opted for the jeep, thinking it would have better traction in the lingering snow. She couldn't wait for spring.

Her thoughts returned to how Russ had called early that morning to cancel their date. Not only was it Valentine's Day, but it was also her birthday. It hurt that he considered anything more important than that.

In the past months they had grown so much closer, and she had hopes their relationship would soon advance to the next step. When Heath proposed to Jane at Christmas, Val had been happy for them but wished it were her and Russ. She longed to be his wife and in time the mother of his children. She'd been at his side when he committed his life to Christ. Her entire family had celebrated his baptism with him.

That night over dinner he'd explained that the baptism was his outward expression of the man in Christ he planned to become.

Russ's determination to do things right meant growing in his relationship with God as well as with her. Val knew his relationship with God would strengthen theirs as well.

God was definitely hard at work in their lives. She was thankful Randall King had not taken any action against Russ. He'd been able to use his time with the firm when he applied to take his exam. Val had been so happy when he told her he'd passed. They had discussed his opening a business in Paris but made no final decision.

Russ and Wendell had talked and Val was happy his brother hadn't turned him away. Val felt confident they would eventually heal their relationship. She wasn't as sure about the relationship between Opie and Wendell. Her sister admitted to caring deeply for Wendell and Val wished she'd never taken her to the bachelor auction.

Glad they had restructured the entrance to the colonnade so it no longer required gates, Val drove up as close as possible and climbed out.

She noted that the lighting wasn't typical. It looked more like a canopy of twinkling lights over the ironwork. Had Jane forgotten to tell her the area was booked for the evening? Probably by a romantic out to impress his girl.

Val patted her pockets and realized she'd left her cell phone at the house. She couldn't even call and ask. She decided to check out the situation before putting someone in the dark.

At the top of the steps, she paused, puzzled by the sight of a single table and chair, a long red rose, and Russ wearing a tuxedo. "What's going on?" she asked, looking around.

"I see you drove out in our chariot," Russ said, indicating the jeep. They had laughed together when Val admitted she had intentionally used the jeep that day. He held out his hand. "Please join me."

"I can't," she whispered. "Opie's waiting at the house."

If his smile hadn't given away that Opie was in on this, his words told Val. "Oh, I don't think she'll have a problem if you don't come back right away."

"What's going on, Russ?"

He took her hand and led her over to the chair draped with a faux fur lap blanket. After seating her, Russ pulled her coat closed and tucked another blanket about her legs. He reached for the rose. "For you, my sweet."

He had been busy. Not only had he strung hundreds of lights, he'd also cleared the pavilion floor of snow and ice. He must have spent the day out here setting up his surprise. Now she understood why Opie had kept her away from home. A gust of wind hit them, and Val shivered. "It's freezing out here."

"I know. We'll go inside soon. Happy Valentine's Day, my Valentine. Forgive me?"

"I thought you forgot."

"Never," he said with a big smile. "Because of you, Valentine's Day will always be a favorite celebration in my life."

"It is hard to forget Valentine's Day when you love someone," she told Russ. "You hurt my feelings when you cancelled our date."

"I know, and I'm truly sorry, but I had to do it to carry out my special plans." Taking her hands in his, Russ said, "When we first met last spring, I had no idea how much I would come to love you."

Tears filled her eyes with his declaration of love. It thrilled her to hear him say the words.

"You've been a true blessing in my life, Val. Before we met I was content with my life of sin; but now I know what it is to be loved by Jesus, and I'll never accept anything less again."

He knelt on a tiny footstool at her feet. "I owe you for leading me along the right path. If you hadn't shared your faith I might never have realized how lost I truly was."

Val wrapped her arms about his neck and hugged him tightly.

He maintained that hold. "I know you're wondering why I brought you out into the cold tonight."

She nodded and hiccupped slightly. "We thought someone left the lights on accidentally."

"No accident. Only the best of intentions," he promised.

"Russ?" His name came out as a mere whisper.

He pulled back and focused on her. "I chose the place that has been significant in our relationship to ask you something very important. The pavilion drew us together in a way no other place ever could. We overcame great obstacles here.

"I came to appreciate the beauty you wanted me to see from day one. But I found something far more beautiful here at Sheridan Farm, Val. Far more incredible than Kentucky farmland, thoroughbreds, and rolling hills. I found you."

"Oh, Russ."

He touched his finger to her lips when she started to say more. "I know I haven't been easy to work with. Probably even frustrating at times; but after I understood, I only became more determined to make you happy.

"When all those crazy things started happening, I became afraid for you and for the family I'd come to love. I never want anything bad to happen to any of you.

"You irritated me when you refused to side with me about Wendell, but once the truth came out I knew I'd been wrong. I'm thankful to have my brother back in my life. I owe that to you, Val.

"You've helped me understand how money can be both a blessing and a burden. I'll never look at worldly possessions in the same way now that I have heaven as my ultimate destination."

She shivered, and he pulled her closer. "I know, talk faster," he teased.

Russ pulled a blue velvet jeweler's box from his pocket. "I love you with all my heart, Valentine Truelove. Will you do me the honor of becoming my wife?"

"Oh, Russ." She sounded like a broken record.

"I don't hear a yes in there."

She took his face in her hands and said

yes each of the three times she kissed him.

He slipped the ring on her finger, and Val admired the heart-shaped diamond with two hearts of smaller diamonds curved along the sides.

"I hope you don't plan to make me wait too long."

"Is June soon enough?" she asked. "After all, we already have the perfect venue, and I know the ideal wedding planner and caterer. And there just happens to be one weekend open in Your Wedding Place's schedule."

"I always wanted a June bride," he declared before kissing her soundly. "Come with me. I have another surprise."

He summoned the lift, and they went to the lower floor where she found the room filled with their family and friends. She looked at him and smiled. "You were awfully confident. What if I'd said no?"

"I wasn't confident at all," Russ admitted. "If you refused, you had a Valentine-themed birthday party. If you said yes, it became a Valentine-themed birthday/engagement party. Opie even made two cakes just in case."

"Oh, there was no way I was going to let you get away once you popped the question," Val said with a laugh.

Russ pulled her into his arms and kissed her.

Opie pushed her way through the crowd, Wendell in her wake. "Did you say yes?"

Val held up her hand. "You know I did."

"You did good," Opie commented, clapping her future brother-in-law on the back.

"Thanks for sending her out," Russ said.

"We weren't sure how to get you out here," Opie explained. "The lights did the trick."

"Congratulations," Wendell said, hugging Val and then his brother.

Their closeness brought tears to her eyes. "Where are Mom and Dad?" Val asked, looking around. Her gaze followed Opie's pointing finger as she indicated the far side of the room. "Do they know?"

Opie nodded. "They're pleased with your choice."

"Me, too," Russ declared with a grin.

She grasped his hand in hers and pulled him over to where her parents stood.

"She said yes."

"I thought she might," Jacob Truelove said. "Russ asked my permission a while back. I said it was up to you, but both your mother and I approve of your choice. Russ is a fine young man."

Val looked at him through tear-filled eyes. "He's the answer to a prayer."

Eighteen

"Ready?"

Unable to push any words past the emotion that blocked her throat, Val nodded.

When she'd talked with her mother about both parents escorting her down the aisle, Cindy Truelove refused.

"Your dad has always looked forward to walking his girls to their future husbands. Let's not take that away from him."

Val understood. She felt that same love for Russ.

Nervous excitement filled him as Russ glanced over at Wendell at the baby grand piano and grinned. Over the past months he'd developed a definite appreciation for his future wife's love of weddings. The planning sessions had gone on forever, and today things had fallen into place with the precision of a well-orchestrated production.

When Val stepped forward, Russ felt as

though his heart would leap from his chest. Cinderella couldn't have been more beautiful. The sun sparkled off the crystals in her tiara and the gold overlay of the white wedding dress.

Her father's proud bearing showed his enjoyment of the day, and more than ever Russ felt honored to become part of this family. Jacob placed Val's hand in his, and they walked to where the minister waited beneath the pavilion.

They shared a smile of joy when the man bowed his head and said, "Let us pray."

AUTHOR'S NOTE:

Typically, in fiction, when the author wants a character to have lots of money, they write their character into someone's will. When I started my "what if?" for something unique, I thought about someone telling me they had given lottery tickets as gifts, and asked myself how most Christians would deal with innocently winning the lottery.

As Christians, we often have a more conservative outlook toward the temptations of life. I, personally, have concerns with the lottery on many levels; so you might ask why I wrote this story.

Because I realized it could happen. Even though some of us choose not to expend funds on games of chance, millions of people do. What if someone gifted you with a winning lottery ticket? Would you be prepared for the outcome? Do you think it possible God could answer your prayers for financial help in such a way?

Val prayed and believed God would answer her prayers. She worked hard, and her boss rewarded her with a gift that made her a wealthy woman. What should she have done? Do we judge her harshly because she chose to be a good steward of the funds she felt God provided? What if it happened to someone you know?

In the story, Val worries about people judging her for the choice she made, and yet when she's confronted with the doubts about Russ, she judges him wrongly. Later, when she realizes what she's done, she seeks his forgiveness and grows in her service to God.

I truly felt the guiding hand of God in the creation of this story. It made me think, and I've had conversations with people about gambling that I would never have had otherwise.

My prayer is that if anyone is struggling with this addictive lifestyle and reads this book, they will understand that God loves them just as they are, and He can change their lives if they will only trust Him.

Terry Fowler

ABOUT THE AUTHOR

Terry Fowler is a native Tarheel who loves calling coastal North Carolina home. Single, she works full-time and is active in her small church. Her greatest pleasure comes from the way God has used her writing to share His message. Her hobbies include gardening, crafts, and genealogical research. Terry invites everyone to visit her Web site at terry fowler.net.